Enid Blyton

BRER RABBIT'S A RASCAL

Enid Blyton

BRER RABBIT'S A RASCAL

DEAN

EGMONT
We bring stories to life

First published in Great Britain in 1965
This edition published in 2007 by Dean,
an imprint of Egmont UK Limited
239 Kensington High Street, London W8 6SA

Copyright © Enid Blyton Limited

Enid Blyton's signature is a registered trademark of Enid Blyton Limited,
a Chorion company.

ISBN 978 0 6035 6283 9

1 3 5 7 9 10 8 6 4 2

Printed in Singapore

CONTENTS

Brer Rabbit's a Rascal!

Now, ONCE WHEN Brer Rabbit was hard at work scraping the stones off his bit of ground, he heard a cry for help. Off he went, rake in hand, to see what the matter was.

It was the little girl belonging to the farmer. She had been fishing in the river and had slipped and fallen in. "Save me," she cried, and went swirling past Brer Rabbit, her skirt spreading out on the water.

Well, old Brer Rabbit he ran beside her, jabbing with his rake. And at last he got hold of the little girl's belt and hauled her to the bank. There she sat, sobbing and crying, her arms round Brer Rabbit's neck.

"You come home to your Ma," said Brer Rabbit. "You're wet. She'll dry you and give you a good hot drink."

So off they went together, the little girl clinging to Brer Rabbit as if she would never let him go. And my word, when the farmer heard how he had saved his little girl there wasn't anything he wouldn't have done for old Brer Rabbit.

"There's a sack of carrots over there," he said. "Take it. And there's a sack of potatoes, too. You're welcome to it. And while you're about it, help yourself to a sack of turnips. You're a born rascal, Brer Rabbit, but you're good-hearted, so you are! Now off you go while I still think good things of you!"

Now, when Brer Rabbit was wheeling home his three sacks, whistling a merry song and feeling on top of the world, who should come along but Brer Fox, Brer Bear and Brer Wolf. How they stared when they saw Brer Rabbit with so much food!

"Carrots! Turnips! Potatoes! Sacks of them!" said Brer Fox. "Hey, Brer Rabbit, give us some. And don't tell us you've come by them honestly, because we shan't believe you!"

Brer Rabbit was most annoyed. "You go and ask the farmer!" he said. "He gave me them with kind words, so he did!"

"Now you're telling stories," said Brer Wolf. "You give us some of those carrots and turnips and potatoes, Brer Rabbit—or we'll come along one night and help ourselves!"

"I *might* have given you some," said Brer Rabbit, wheeling his barrow away with his head in the air. "I *might* have given you some if you knew how to behave!"

Brer Bear, Brer Fox and Brer Wolf stared after Brer Rabbit. Brer Fox scratched his head. "Well, however he got those sacks he's going to share them with us, whether he wants to or not! Shall we go along to his place tonight and see where he's put the sacks?"

"Yes," said the other two, and Brer Fox grinned at them. "Meet me here. We'll slip along in the shadows—and my, won't Brer Rabbit be angry in the morning!"

Now, old Brer Rabbit had a kind of feeling that Brer Fox, Brer Wolf and Brer Bear might be along that night. He wheeled his sacks to his shed and he emptied all the carrots, potatoes and turnips out on the ground. He picked out the bad ones and set them aside. Then he took a big broom and swept all the roots along the ground to his cellar.

Bumpity-bumpity-bump—they rolled down into his cellar and he shut and locked the door. Then he went back to the shed again. He took the sacks to the pile of stones he had scraped off his ground and he filled them almost to the top with the stones. But right at the very top he didn't put the stones—he put a layer of bad carrots, a layer of poor potatoes, and in the third sack a layer of rotten turnips. Oh, Brer Rabbit, you're a wily one!

He dragged the sacks back to his shed and set them up against the walls. Then he went indoors, leaving the shed door unlocked.

"And if this isn't a nice easy way of getting rid of all those stones, well, I'll never know a better one!" said old Brer Rabbit.

Now, that night along crept Brer Fox, Brer Bear and Brer Wolf. There was a little moon so they kept well in the shadows. They came to the shed and tried the door. It wasn't locked—that was fine!

They slipped inside. Brer Bear pointed to the three sacks in glee. He looked in the top of one. He could see dimly in the moonlight—and he saw potatoes!

"Here are the potatoes," he said. "I'll take this sack. You follow with the others, Brer Wolf and Brer Fox."

They staggered out with the sacks. "My sack is mighty heavy!" said Brer Fox, groaning. "I never thought turnips could be such a dreadful weight."

"These carrots are heavy, too," panted Brer Wolf. "My, they must be good solid ones!"

Brer Rabbit saw the three of them through his window, staggering up the lane in the shadows. He grinned to himself. "Nice of them to carry those tiresome stones away!" he said. "I must thank them when I see them!"

Well, by the time Brer Fox, Brer Wolf and Brer Bear had reached their homes they couldn't walk a step farther! They sank down on the ground, panting. Brer Bear thought he would make some potato soup and he shook the sack hard—and out came six poor potatoes—and about twenty big stones!

Then Brer Bear knew he had been tricked and he rushed to tell Brer Fox and Brer Wolf. But they had already found out, and dear me, the names they called old Brer Rabbit would have made his whiskers curl if he had heard them!

Brer Rabbit went out of his way to meet the three the next day. He raised his hat politely and gave his very best bow.

"My best thanks, gentlemen, for so kindly removing all those stones for me," he said. "I shall have another sackful tomorrow if one of you would like to call for it."

And then, my goodness me, he had to run for his life—but he didn't mind that because Brer Rabbit could always run faster than anyone else. As for Brer Bear, Brer Wolf and Brer Fox, they had to carry all the stones out of their gardens and empty them into the ditch. They were so stiff afterwards that they couldn't walk properly for days!

Ah, Brer Rabbit, it's hard to get the better of you, you rascal!

You Can't Trick Brer Rabbit!

IT HAPPENED ONCE that Brer Fox thought of a good way to catch Brer Rabbit for his dinner. He waited until he saw Brer Rabbit coming along down the lane, and then he set up a mighty groaning and limped along as if one of his legs were badly hurt.

"Ooh my, ooh my!" he groaned, pretending that he didn't see Brer Rabbit. "I'm sure I shan't get home! My leg's broken, that's certain!"

He suddenly fell down on the ground, and lay there making a great hullabaloo. Brer Rabbit stopped a little way behind him in surprise.

"What's got you, Brer Fox?" he asked.

"I've just broken my leg," said Brer Fox. "You come and help me home, Brer Rabbit, there's a good fellow. Give me your arm, for I can't walk alone. You mustn't leave me here like this, for I'd die. I can't walk another step!"

But Brer Rabbit wasn't easily tricked. "You wait there, Brer Fox," he said. "I'll get help for you."

"But I'll die before you bring help," said Brer Fox, making a great moaning noise again. "You come along and help me now, Brer Rabbit."

"I'll go and get you something to eat, first," said Brer Rabbit. "That will get your strength up so's you'll be able to walk with me."

"That's kind of you, Brer Rabbit," said Brer Fox. So off went Brer Rabbit. Nearby was Brer Bear's house, and Brer Rabbit knew he had been baking a meat-pie that day. He saw that Brer Bear had put it on the window-sill to cool. He snatched it up and ran off to Brer Fox with it.

"Here you are, Brer Fox," he said. "You eat that up and you'll feel better. I'll be back in two shakes of a duck's tail to help you home."

Brer Fox took the pie greedily and began to gobble it up. Brer Rabbit rushed back to Brer Bear's house and banged on the door, crying, "Heyo, Brer Bear! Have you lost a fine meat-pie? There's old Brer Fox a-sitting down the lane, and he's gobbling up a pie as fast as he can!"

Brer Bear went to the window-sill to see if his pie were there, and when he saw it was gone, he shouted in a fearful rage.

"Stars and moon! It's gone. I'll bite Brer Fox's head off for that!"

Off he ran out into the lane, grunting and growling most fearsomely. "Oy, oy, yi, yi, where's Brer Fox? I'll bite his head off! I'll gobble his tail! I'll cook his whiskers! Where's my meat-pie?"

As soon as Brer Fox heard this awful noise and saw Brer Bear pounding down the lane he turned pale with fright. He threw the pie into the hedge and leapt to his feet.

"You mind your broken leg, Brer Fox!" yelled Brer Rabbit, laughing fit to kill himself. "You mind that broken leg!"

But Brer Fox didn't wait to think of his leg. No, it had mended itself all in a hurry, and you couldn't see him for dust! As for old Brer Rabbit, he took the pie out of the hedge and sat down to enjoy it. It's a pity to waste anything, isn't it?

A Happy New Year!

DID YOU EVER hear the tale of how Brer Fox and Brer Wolf planned to break into Brer Rabbit's house one night and steal all the little fat youngsters there?

"We'll make him tear his whiskers and dance with fury!" grinned Brer Fox. "Ho, ho! What will he say when he finds all his young ones gone one morning? He'll think twice before he plays a joke on *us* again!"

"We'd better choose a very dark night when there is no moon at all," said Brer Wolf. "In two weeks from now, shall we say? Very well, Brer Fox. Meet me outside Brer Rabbit's gate in the middle of the night—and we'll have a fine time!"

So on the night planned Brer Fox and Brer Wolf met silently outside Brer Rabbit's gate. It was about ten minutes to

midnight—and to Brer Fox's enormous surprise there was a
bright light in Brer Rabbit's parlour! There was also a great
noise of shouting, laughing and dancing.

"Strange!" said Brer Fox, puzzled. "He must be having a
party. I say, Brer Wolf, let's hide under a bush in the garden, and
jump on the guests as they come out! Brer Hare and his family
are sure to be there, and all Brer Rabbit's cousins. We shall have
a fine feast!"

So into the garden they crept and squatted under a bush.

Now Brer Rabbit certainly *was* having a party! You see, it was
New Year's Eve, and he meant to see in the New Year with all
his friends. They were very happy indeed, and most excited.

"Let's welcome the New Year in at midnight with as much
noise as we can," said Brer Rabbit. "That would be fun! Here,
Brer Terrapin, you can have a couple of saucepans to bang if you
like—and you, Brer Turkey-Buzzard, can borrow my frying
pans."

"I'll have the dinner-bell," said Brer Frog, leaping down from the curtain at last. "And *I'll* take the pail from under the sink and bang it with the rolling-pin," said Brer Bear, happily. "And *I'll* have the old tin tray," said Brer Hare. "Oh, yes, and the shovel, too—my, I'll make a fine din!"

Well, just at midnight, when the clock was striking twelve, Brer Rabbit threw open his front door, and all his guests streamed out to welcome in the New Year, carrying with them the saucepans, frying-pans, dinner-bell, pail and tray. Brer Fox and Brer Wolf, who were waiting patiently under their bush, leapt out at once, thinking that their chance had come—but, stars and moon, what was all this? Crash, clang, ding, clonk, smash, bang, crash, ding, clonk ... all the guests began to bang together their saucepans, pans and pails, and Brer Fox and Brer Wolf stopped still in horror and alarm! They were terrified out of their lives!

Brer Rabbit saw them in the light that came from his parlour, and in a trice he knew they were up to something. "Come on, boys!" he shouted to his guests. "Wish them a Happy New Year!"

Then, to Brer Fox's and Brer Wolf's terror, everyone tore after them, banging, clanking, dinging, crashing for all they were worth, and shouting at the tops of their voices, "A Happy New Year, a Happy New Year!"

"*That's* a good beginning to the year, anyway," said Brer Rabbit, in delight, as he watched Brer Fox and Brer Wolf streak away like lightning. "Come along in again, friends. Happy New Year, everybody!"

Brer Fox and Brer Wolf stopped still in horror and alarm!

Brer Rabbit's New Year Gift

NOW IT HAPPENED once that Brer Fox took to hiding round corners and under bushes and behind fences waiting to spring out at Brer Rabbit whenever he passed, and Brer Rabbit got quite jumpy and upset.

"Now look here, Brer Fox," said Brer Rabbit, "this isn't friendly of you. One of these days you'll scare me out of my skin, and you'll be sorry."

Brer Fox grinned. "It's just what I'm hoping to do," he said. "Once I make you really jump out of your skin, Brer Rabbit, you'll be all ready for the cooking pot."

Well, that didn't please Brer Rabbit at all. He thought for a mighty long time, and then he brightened up. "*I'll* soon stop Brer Fox's tricks!" he said to himself, and off he went to the town. He bought a large watch with a very loud tick. He wrapped it up and sent it through the post with a label inside that said, "To Brer Fox, from an Unknown Friend."

Well, when Brer Fox opened the parcel and found the watch inside, and the message, he was mighty pleased. He put the watch into his waistcoat pocket, and went out to show it to everyone, Brer Rabbit as well.

"My!" said Brer Rabbit, pretending to be most surprised. "That's a beautiful watch, Brer Fox. Just you leave it about, and I'll come and get it. I'd dearly like it myself!"

"Huh!" said Brer Fox. "I shan't leave it about, don't you worry, Brer Rabbit. I shall always wear it and there won't be any chance of you finding it."

Well, that was just what Brer Rabbit wanted, of course! He grinned to himself and did a little dance as soon as Brer Fox was

round the corner. Now he would be able to hear Brer Fox whenever he was anywhere near!

"If he hides behind the fence I shall hear tick-a-tock, tick-a-tock as soon as I come along!" thought Brer Rabbit. "And I'll jump on him, so I will! And if he hides under a bush I'll hear tick-a-tock, tick-a-tock long before I get up to him—and I'll creep round the bush and get hold of his tail! And if he's hiding round a corner, I'll hear tick-a-tock, tick-a-tock, and I'll go round the other way and yell in his ear! My, I'll have a fine time now old Brer Fox has got that watch!"

Well, for some time Brer Fox was so pleased with his watch and went about showing it to so many people that he quite forgot about lying in wait for Brer Rabbit. And when Brer Rabbit met him one morning he said, "Heyo, Brer Fox! I'm glad my skin's safe now! That watch of yours has made you forget your silly tricks."

Now that made Brer Fox think. "Ha!" he said to himself, "maybe it was Brer Rabbit sent me this watch. Maybe it's he who is the Unknown Friend—and he thinks the new watch will make me forget to scare him. Ah, Brer Rabbit, you're sly—but I'm slyer! I'll soon teach you that I'm up to all my tricks, and, tails and whiskers, I'll give you such a scare before the week is out that your hair will stand on end and your bobtail will curl with fright!"

Brer Rabbit watched Brer Fox's face and he guessed his thoughts. He scampered off, lippitty, clippetty, laughing as he went.

Brer Rabbit was too smart to be caught by Brer Fox!

Brer Bear's Eggs

ONCE IT HAPPENED that Brer Bear kept chickens and stored up the eggs in pickle so that he could use them in the winter-time. Brer Rabbit got to hear of this, and he licked his lips. He trotted round to old Brer Bear's, sat down, and gossiped with him. Soon he led Brer Bear to talk of his eggs, and Brer Rabbit said, "And how many eggs have you put away, Brer Bear?"

"I don't know," said Brer Bear. "I can't count more than five."

"Oh, that's bad," said Brer Rabbit. "*I'll* count them for you, if you like. Show me where the eggs are."

So Brer Bear showed him. They were locked up in a shed. Brer Rabbit counted them over and there were 40.

"Suppose somebody steals some," said Brer Rabbit, "how are you going to know?"

"I *shan't* know!" said Brer Bear, sorrowfully.

"Well, look here," said Brer Rabbit. "If you like, I'll come along and count them for you every day, Brer Bear. Then you'll know if the number is all right."

"Thank you, Brer Rabbit," said Brer Bear, gratefully. So each morning Brer Rabbit scampered along to Brer Bear's lippitty, clippetty—but instead of counting them, the wicked creature took an egg for himself every day!

Well, after thirty-nine days there was only one egg left. Brer Rabbit arrived that morning to find Brer Fox sitting with Brer Bear. When Brer Fox heard that Brer Rabbit was counting Brer Bear's eggs for him each morning, he threw back his head and laughed uncontrollably.

"Ho! Brer Bear, you don't suppose you've got your forty eggs there *now*, do you?" he said. "Brer Rabbit doesn't do these good deeds for nothing. Not he!"

Brer Bear was worried—but he didn't like to think such things of Brer Rabbit. As for Brer Rabbit, he looked very hurt, and spoke humbly to Brer Bear.

"Oh, Brer Bear," he said. "I hope you won't listen to Brer Fox. Let me go into the shed, and I will bring out your eggs and show you there are forty."

"Very well," said Brer Bear. So into the shed hopped Brer Rabbit, took up the one egg there, marked a figure 1 on it, and went out to show it to Brer Bear and Brer Fox. Then back he went, licked the figure 1 off, and wrote the figure 2 on the egg. He ran out and showed it to Brer Bear.

"Number 2 egg!" he said. Then back he went, licked off the 2 and wrote 3 instead. And so the wicked rascal went on until he had reached number 40—but all the time he only showed the same one egg, and neither Brer Bear nor Brer Fox knew it. Brer

18

Bear was pleased to think he had his 40 eggs safe, and he said so. "Brer Rabbit, you can have that last egg for your trouble!" he said. So Brer Rabbit put the egg into his pocket, said goodbye, and ran off, grinning.

But Brer Fox saw that grin—and he went and looked in the shed to see the other eggs—and found none there! Then he knew the trick that Brer Rabbit had played, and he told Brer Bear he'd go along to Brer Rabbit's house and see if he could find the eggs for him. But Brer Rabbit saw him coming, broke all the eggs into a jug of milk and drank them up!

Six of the eggs were bad—and Brer Rabbit lay in bed for three days, groaning, for he had a dreadful pain.

"When bad habits and bad eggs go together, there's sure to be a bad pain!" said Brer Fox. "Serves you right, Brer Rabbit!"

Bobs Meets Brer Rabbit

ONCE UPON A TIME Bobs the dog buried a very large bone in the farmer's field of carrots. He thought it would be safe there—but it wasn't! For one night who should come along that way, digging up carrots, but old Brer Rabbit—and, of course, he found Bobs' bone.

"My!" said Brer Rabbit, "here's a bone to make soup. I'll have carrot-and-bone soup tonight, so I will!" He tucked the bone in his pocket, and set off down the lane. But he hadn't gone far before he met Bobs ambling along—and Bobs smelt the bone at once!

"Fine smell of bone about," he said to Brer Rabbit. "Can *you* smell it, Brer Rabbit?"

"*Bone!*" said Brer Rabbit, pretending to be surprised. "*Bone*, Bobs! Don't be silly. You can smell the bone in your leg, that's what you can smell!"

But Bobs knew better. He looked at Brer Rabbit and saw his bulging pockets. So he was mighty polite and chatted away to Brer Rabbit as if he had known him for years.

"You come along to my kennel and see what a fine big house I've got!" said Bobs. "I may have some biscuits there."

So Brer Rabbit trotted beside Bobs, and the two of them went lippitty-clippetty to Old Thatch. Bobs led Brer Rabbit to his big kennel. Brer Rabbit, sniffing for biscuits, hopped in and Bobs banged the door and bolted it! Aha, Brer Rabbit, you're caught now!

"Let me out, Bobs," said Brer Rabbit. "I'll escape if you don't, and I shan't be friends with you any more!"

"You can't escape from there!" said Bobs, with a grin so wide that his whiskers nearly fell off. "I'm going to tell Sandy about you!"

But he didn't go to tell Sandy. No, Bobs had a better plan than that! He slipped off to the gardener's shed, where he remembered seeing the gardener's old cap and old red scarf hanging! He put the cap on his head, and twisted the scarf round his neck. Then he woofed to himself in glee! Old Brer Rabbit was going to be properly tricked! He ran back to the kennel, but when he got near he began to whistle as if he were just someone passing by. Brer Rabbit looked out of the window of the kennel and saw him—but he didn't know it was Bobs, of course!

"Heyo, friend!" said Brer Rabbit. "Aren't you mighty cold out there tonight?"

"Very cold!" said Bobs, in a funny deep voice. "You are lucky to have a warm house to sleep in, I can tell you!"

"Well, I do feel so sorry for you, that I will lend you my house to sleep in this cold night," said Brer Rabbit, pretending to be very kind.

"You just open the door, friend, and you can sleep here with me."

21

"I want something to eat first," said Bobs, "I'm so very hungry!"

"Well, take this bone and these carrots," said Brer Rabbit, pushing them through the window. "And now just open the door, and you can come in and snooze on the straw."

Bobs took the bone and the carrots and grinned. He unbolted the door of the kennel—and Brer Rabbit shot out. "Tell Bobs I've escaped after all!" he shouted.

"Oh, he knows that all right!" called Bobs, in his own voice. "Thanks for leaving me the bone and the carrots, Brer Rabbit! I won't ask you to stay and share them!"

Pull his Ears, Brer Fox!

NOW ONCE IT HAPPENED that Brer Fox went fishing, and caught a mighty lot of fish. He strung them on a line and carried them proudly through the wood, showing them to everyone he met. Brer Rabbit heard him boasting about them, and he ran to Brer Donkey, who was grazing in a nearby field.

"Come with me," he said to Brer Donkey. "You like a bit of fish, don't you? Well, here's a chance to get some!"

Brer Donkey squeezed through the hedge and went to a big bush of bramble with Brer Rabbit.

"Now you sit yourself down there," said Brer Rabbit to Brer Donkey. "And just stick your ears up straight as soon as I get in beside you. Don't you show anything except your ears, Brer Donkey, and don't you show those till I get in beside you—and go on showing them till you see it's time to stop."

"Just as you say, Brer Rabbit," said Brer Donkey, and he settled himself down at the bottom of the bramble bush.

Now along came Brer Fox, swinging his string of fish, and humming a little song. Out stepped Brer Rabbit and bid him "How do you do?"

"That's a mighty fine string of fish you've got," said Brer Rabbit, staring hard at it.

"Yes," said Brer Fox. "Would you like to hear how I caught them all?"

"I would," said Brer Rabbit. "But I'm not sitting beside you, Brer Fox. Oh, no! You're not going to have rabbit-pie for dinner!"

"And you're not going to have fish for dinner," said Brer Fox, looking mighty cautious. "You just sit down in front of me, Brer

Rabbit, where I can see you—and I'm going to hang my fish *behind* me, over this branch."

"That suits me all right," said Brer Rabbit, and he skipped into the bramble bush beside Brer Donkey.

"Stick your ears up so that I can see you," said Brer Fox, and at the same moment old Brer Donkey stuck up his hairy ears and twitched them about. Brer Fox took a glance at them, and reckoned they were Brer Rabbit's ears all right. And he began the long, long tale of how he caught his fish. Brer Donkey twitched his ears all the time as if he were listening hard—but old Brer Rabbit, he crept out of the bramble bush, dashed down a hole nearby and came up just behind Brer Fox. And it wasn't long before that string of fish slipped from the branch where it hung—and disappeared down the burrow too.

Then Brer Rabbit popped up into the bramble bush

again, giggling like a green woodpecker. "Heyo, Brer Fox, watch your fish!" he called. Brer Fox turned round—and saw that his fish were gone! And in the same moment old Brer Donkey set down his ears, and Brer Rabbit set his up—and out he walked, ears and all, in front of Brer Fox.

"I suppose you'll say I took your fish, Brer Fox?" he said, with a grin.

"Well, you didn't," said Brer Fox. "I saw your ears a-listening to me all the time. Ah, wait till I catch that thief!"

But when he passed by Brer Rabbit's house that night, and smelt the smell of frying fish, and saw Brer Donkey and Brer Rabbit having a good tuck-in, Brer Fox was mighty puzzled. But he wasn't puzzled any more when Brer Donkey stuck his head out of the window, twitched his hairy ears, and cried, "That was a mighty fine tale of yours about the fish, Brer Fox, a mighty fine tale."

Brer Rabbit Gets Caught

DID YOU EVER HEAR how Brer Rabbit got caught by Brer Fox, and was marched off over the fields? Well, it happened that Brer Rabbit was busy scrabbling for carrots, and didn't hear Brer Fox creeping up—and suddenly there was a pounce and a shout, and there was Brer Rabbit properly caught by the fur at the back of his neck!

"Ooh-ow!" said Brer Rabbit in a fright.

"Aha!" said Brer Fox. "I've really got you this time, Brer Rabbit—yes, there's no doubt about it at all. And you're going home with me. Come along!"

So they went along and they went along, Brer Rabbit racking his brains for some way of escape. At last he began to puff and pant in a most alarming manner.

"What's the matter, Brer Rabbit?" said Brer Fox, surprised.

"Oh, Brer Fox, please, sir, you go so fast!" said Brer Rabbit. "You've such long legs, I can't keep up with you. I'll be nothing but skin and bone by the time I get to your house if you hurry me along like this."

Well, Brer Fox much preferred Brer Rabbit to be plump, and not skin and bone, so he went more slowly. But Brer Rabbit still panted as if he had been running a mile.

"Oh, Brer Fox, please, sir, could we have a rest for a minute?" begged Brer Rabbit in a humble voice. "Just a little small rest. Look, there's a nice little hillock of grass I could sit on for a moment. And there's a nice hard stone for you."

"Huh!" said Brer Fox, in disgust. "*I'll* take the grassy hillock

and *you* can have the hard stone, Brer Rabbit. You can have a
very little small rest."

So Brer Rabbit sat on the stone, and Brer Fox sat on the
hillock of grass—which, as Brer Rabbit knew very well indeed,
was nothing but an ant-hill. Yes, a fine big ant-hill where red
stinging ants lived, and mighty angry they were to have their
precious city sat upon so hard!

"It's good of you to give me a rest, Brer Fox," said Brer
Rabbit. "But don't you take your hand away from the back of
my neck, or I might escape. You hold me tight."

"You don't need to tell me that," said Brer Fox, scornfully.
Brer Rabbit watched a dozen ants run up Brer Fox's fur—then a
dozen more, and then a hundred! Brer Fox put up his back leg
and scratched himself because the ants tickled. Then they began
to bite him, and he put up both hind legs and rubbed hard.
Then they bit him everywhere, for they were angry with him for

sitting on their town. Brer Fox gave a great yell and leapt up into the air.

"I'm sitting on an ant-hill!" he howled. "Ooh! They're all over me! They're biting and stinging me!"

Well, those ants gave poor Brer Fox such a bad time that he hadn't any paw left to hold Brer Rabbit—he wanted all four of his paws to deal with the angry ants! And soon he was leaping high into the air and then rolling on the ground scratching and yelling for all he was worth.

Well, you may be sure Brer Rabbit didn't stay to watch him! No—he was off down the nearest rabbit-hole with a flash of his white bobtail. But he was mighty careful after that not to scrabble for carrots when Brer Fox was anywhere about!

Brer Wolf's Dinner Party

ONCE BRER WOLF thought he would give a dinner party. So he asked Brer Rabbit, Brer Hare and Brer Turkey Buzzard to come, and also Brer Fox and Brer Bear.

Brer Hare was delighted. He didn't often go to parties. Brer Turkey Buzzard had been to one, and had never forgotten it because he had eaten so many ices. He longed to go to another. Only Brer Rabbit didn't seem too glad about the party.

It wasn't like Brer Wolf to give a party. He was a mean old thing who wouldn't even waste his breath to blow a hot pudding. Brer Rabbit puzzled his brains about it—and then he began to hang about Brer Wolf's house to see what things were being sent for the party.

But no matter how much Brer Rabbit watched, he couldn't see a thing arriving at Brer Wolf's! Well, maybe he was going to cook the dinner all himself then.

So Brer Rabbit hid under a bush and watched Brer Wolf's chimney to see if a great amount of smoke came out of it, which would show he was having a mighty big cooking-fire. But no, only a wisp of smoke showed—Brer Wolf couldn't even be boiling an egg!

Brer Rabbit didn't like the look of things at all. On the day of the party he met Brer Hare and Brer Turkey Buzzard, both dressed up in their best, and they went towards Brer Wolf's house. "Wait here a moment," said Brer Rabbit at the gate. He tiptoed towards the house and looked in at the window. He saw the table laid all ready—but it was set with three plates only, and three knives and forks. A great pot of boiling water hung over the fire, and an empty dish was warming by the flames.

Three plates—and six guests! Brer Rabbit knew what *that* meant all right! He poked his head in at the window and saw Brer Wolf, Brer Fox and Brer Bear all hiding behind the door.

"Heyo!" said Brer Rabbit, cheerfully. "What are you all doing there, hiding like that?"

"We're—er—we're just playing a game of hide-and-seek till you come," said Brer Wolf, hurriedly.

"And why are there only three plates on the table?" asked Brer Rabbit, grinning.

"Well—somehow I'm not hungry, and nor are Brer Fox and Brer Bear," said Brer Wolf. "So we've just laid for you and the others, you see."

"And what are we to eat?" asked Brer Rabbit, looking all round the kitchen.

"It's a s-s-surprise," stammered Brer Wolf.

"And *I've* got a surprise for *you*, too," said Brer Rabbit, with his most cheerful grin. "I and my friends aren't hungry either, so we won't visit you today, thank you very much. Hope you'll feel hungry this evening—I rather think you will!"

And with that Brer Rabbit skipped off with Brer Hare and Brer Turkey Buzzard—and that was the last of Brer Wolf's party!

Brer Rabbit and Brer Turkey Buzzard

IT HAPPENED ONCE that Brer Fox chased after Brer Rabbit and got so close to him that all Brer Rabbit could do was to run into a hollow tree. The hole was too small for Brer Fox to get in after him, so Brer Fox lay down to get his breath.

While he was lying there, Brer Turkey Buzzard came flapping along and thought Brer Fox was dead.

"Brer Fox is dead, and I'm so sorry!" he said.

"No, I'm not dead," said Brer Fox. "I've got old man Rabbit penned up in this tree. You sit and keep guard, Brer Turkey Buzzard, and I'll go and get my axe to chop down the tree."

Well, Brer Fox loped off and Brer Buzzard stood by the tree-hole. By and by, when all was still, Brer Rabbit began to scramble about inside the tree, and shouted out, "Brer Fox! Brer Fox!"

Nobody said anything. Brer Fox was gone. Then Brer Rabbit shouted like mad and said, "You needn't talk if you don't want to, Brer Fox! I wish mighty bad that Brer Buzzard was here!"

Then Brer Buzzard tried to talk like Brer Fox. "What do you want with Brer Buzzard?" he said.

"Oh, nothing much, except that there's the very fattest grey squirrel in here that ever I did see!" said Brer Rabbit. "If Brer Buzzard was here, I'd drive him out of a little hole at the back of this tree and he could catch him easily."

"Drive him out, then," said Brer Buzzard, "and I'll see that Brer Buzzard gets him!"

And with that Brer Buzzard slipped round to the other side of the tree.

Then Brer Rabbit shot out of the other hole and set out for home! As for old Brer Buzzard, he reckoned he would stay and

watch Brer Fox chop down the tree all for nothing! So he waited. And presently along came Brer Fox with his axe.

"How's Brer Rabbit getting on?" said Brer Fox. "Oh, he's in there, he's in there!" said Brer Buzzard. "He's very still, though. Perhaps he's taking a nap!"

"Well, I'm just in time to wake him up!" said Brer Fox, and he began to chop the tree. And every time he brought his axe down—pow!—on the tree old Brer Buzzard did a little dance and shouted out, "Oh, he's in there, Brer Fox, sure! He's in there!"

Well, Brer Fox lammed away at that hollow tree, and when he had got it half cut through he suddenly caught sight of Brer Buzzard laughing at him behind his back! Then he knew something was up, and he went and peeped inside the hole of the tree.

"Look here, Brer Buzzard!" he called. "Come and see if this isn't Brer Rabbit's foot hanging down here!"

Then Brer Buzzard hopped up and stuck his head in the hole—and Brer Fox grabbed hold of him, and there he was, caught.

"So you've tricked me, have you?" said Brer Fox. "Well, I left you here to watch Brer Rabbit—and I come back and find him gone! I'm going to settle you right now, Brer Buzzard!" said Brer Fox.

With that he took hold of Brer Buzzard by the tail, meaning to dash him on the ground—but it was just about the time of year that Brer Buzzard moulted—so all his tail feathers came out in Brer Fox's hand, and Brer Buzzard sailed away into the air like a balloon. And as he went he shouted, "You've given me a good start, Brer Fox!" And Brer Fox—he sat and watched him fly out of sight!

Brer Rabbit's Fence

BRER RABBIT'S FENCE was in a very bad way. It wanted painting, there was no doubt about that! Brer Rabbit went to have a look at it and groaned.

"I've tooth-ache in one arm and ear-ache in the other!" he said. "How can I paint all that long fence!"

However, it had to be done, so he got a can of paint and began. Slish-slosh, slish-slosh went his brush, to and fro. Presently along came Brer Bear.

"That's a fine sloshy job you're doing," he said to Brer Rabbit. "Could I have a turn, do you think?"

"Certainly, Brer Bear!" said Brer Rabbit, and he gave Brer Bear the brush at once. Slish-slosh, slish-slosh, went Brer Bear very happily. He *was* enjoying himself!

Soon along came Brer Turkey Buzzard, jerking his big head to and fro as he walked. He stood and watched Brer Bear with envy. What a lovely job!

"Brer Rabbit's letting *me* have a turn," said Brer Bear. "Isn't it kind of him?"

"Can *I* have a turn, too?" said Brer Turkey Buzzard.

"Certainly, Brer Turkey Buzzard," said Brer Rabbit, kindly. "Just let Brer Bear finish this bit of fence."

So after a bit Brer Turkey Buzzard took up the brush and began to paint, too. Brer Hare came along and watched, and Brer Fox and Brer Wolf came up arm-in-arm.

"Here, Brer Turkey Buzzard, you're doing that wrong!" said Brer Wolf, and he snatched the brush away. *"This* is how you do it."

Slish-slosh went the brush, and Brer Turkey Buzzard got a big dab of paint in the eye. He let out a squawk, but Brer Wolf took no notice.

"Brer Rabbit, it's *my* turn after Brer Wolf," said Brer Fox, showing all his sharp teeth. Brer Rabbit pretended to look frightened. He nodded his head.

"Y-y-y-yes, Brer F-f-f-fox," he said. "You shall have the next turn—a nice *long* turn, if you like!"

So Brer Fox had a turn next—and a good long turn it was, too! By the time he had finished, the fence was completely painted. Not a bare place was left. It shone as bright as new, and Brer Rabbit was mighty pleased. He had been sitting in an armchair by the window, watching. Dear me, how nice it was to see other people doing his work!

Brer Fox dipped the brush into the can for the last time, and sloshed it down a big post to give it a good coat. "There!" he said. "No one else can have a turn. There's no paint left!"

Everyone stood admiring the fence. Presently Brer Possum strolled up, and how he did gape to see the fence all finished, for it hadn't even been begun when he had passed by that morning.

"Heyo, Brer Rabbit!" he called, seeing Brer Rabbit at the window. "That's pretty quick work! How did you get your fence done so quickly? You must be tired out!"

"Oh no, Brer Possum," called back Brer Rabbit at once. "I'm not a bit tired. I just told my friends to come along here and do the work for me, and they did. Brer Fox did the most. He was afraid I might *bite* him if he didn't work hard!"

And with that Brer Rabbit slammed down his window and laughed till he cried to see everyone's face! As for Brer Fox, he couldn't bear even the *smell* of paint after that!

Brer Rabbit Joins the Party

BRER BEAR WAS GOING to give a party to Brer Fox and Brer Wolf. Brer Rabbit wasn't asked, and he was in a rage about it because he knew Brer Bear was cooking chicken and fish, so it would be a mighty fine feast.

When Brer Bear was cooking for the party Brer Rabbit turned up and asked if he could help him.

"If you like," said Brer Bear, "but you can't come to the party, Brer Rabbit, so don't you think so. Brer Wolf and Brer Fox said they wouldn't come if I asked you too."

Brer Rabbit didn't say anything for a minute, and then he suddenly sniffed at the fish Brer Bear was cooking. "What's the matter?" asked Brer Bear.

"Smells bad to me," said Brer Rabbit. "Of course, it's your own business, Brer Bear, but *I* wouldn't give bad fish to any guests of mine."

"It smells good enough to me," said Brer Bear sniffing at it.

"Well, you give it to Brer Fox and Brer Wolf, then," said Brer Rabbit. "But if I hear of them being mighty ill I'll know who it was poisoned them, Brer Bear."

Brer Bear looked alarmed. "Stars and moon!" he said anxiously. "I wouldn't like to poison them. Maybe I'll eat the fish myself and give the chicken to Brer Fox and Brer Wolf."

"Yes, you do that," said Brer Rabbit. "And see here, Brer Bear, I'll stay and see to the washing-up for you, if you like. I don't want any of the dinner, but I don't mind giving a hand to an old friend when he's got a party."

So Brer Rabbit stayed, and when Brer Fox and Brer Wolf came to the feast he sat down as good as gold in a corner. Brer Bear gave his friends the chicken and began to eat the fish

himself. Brer Rabbit watched him with a very worried look on his face. Brer Bear couldn't help wondering if the fish was bad.

"You're not looking very well, Brer Bear," said Brer Rabbit, all of a sudden. "You look pale and miserable."

Brer Bear felt more and more worried. How dreadful if he were poisoned by the fish Brer Rabbit said was bad! He felt quite upset and pushed his plate away.

"You're not well, Brer Bear," said Brer Rabbit. "You're poisoned by that fish! Poor Brer Bear! You go to the doctor at once, Brer Bear. Brer Fox and Brer Wolf will hold you up if your legs give way."

Brer Bear was terribly frightened. He really did feel as if his legs were giving way. Brer Fox and Brer Wolf got up and held

41

him. Then, groaning and moaning, Brer Bear went off to the doctor, dragged along by Brer Fox and Brer Wolf, who were nearly as frightened as he was.

"I'll look after your dinner for you!" called Brer Rabbit as they went. He grinned to himself, and you should have seen how well he looked after that dinner! First of all he ate up the fish, which was as good as any he had ever had, and then he gobbled up the chicken from Brer Wolf's plate and Brer Fox's dish. Then he washed up and left everything clean. Soon he heard Brer Bear and the others coming back. Brer Bear looked as wild as could be, so Brer Rabbit didn't stay to ask how he was. He just called out "Your dinner's quite all right!" and ran off lippitty, clippitty through the woods, laughing as loudly as a green woodpecker!

Brer Rabbit and the Teapot

NOW ONCE WHEN Brer Rabbit was giving a big tea-party to all his friends and relations, and was busy pouring out cups of tea from an enormous brown teapot, Brer Fox and Brer Bear strolled in.

Well, of course, all the guests fled out of the back door and out of the windows as if a big wind had suddenly blown them away. All except poor Brer Rabbit, and he hadn't time to leap through a window. He only just had time to put the enormous teapot down, jump into it himself, and put on the lid. There he shivered in the teapot, although the tea was hot round his legs!

Brer Fox and Brer Bear leaned against the table, waiting for the guests to come back. "Then we'll pounce on a few," said Brer Fox, "and join the tea-party!"

That made Brer Rabbit as mad as could be! He wriggled a paw down the teapot spout and jabbed Brer Fox hard in the back.

Brer Fox was surprised. He rubbed his back and glared at Brer Bear. "Stop poking me!" he said.

Then Brer Bear looked surprised. "I didn't poke you," he said. Just then Brer Rabbit jiggled the lid up and down and made it say "Jiggle, jiggle, jiggle."

"Don't jiggle the table," said Brer Fox.

"I'm not," said Brer Bear. "It's you!"

Brer Rabbit slipped his paw down the spout again and gave Brer Fox another hard jab. Brer Fox nearly fell on his nose. He shook his fist in Brer Bear's face. "If you jab me again, I'll fight you!" he said. "I didn't bring you here to treat me like this!"

"Jiggle, jiggle, jiggle," said the teapot lid. Then Brer Rabbit poked Brer Bear in his most ticklish spot, and Brer Bear gave a

yell and slapped Brer Fox in the face. "Stop tickling me!" he cried.

Then what a fight there was! How the fur flew over Brer Rabbit's kitchen! How the chairs went over with a crash! Brer Rabbit trembled in the teapot, for he was afraid that the table would be knocked over and the teapot would fall and break. But it didn't.

Brer Fox and Brer Bear stopped for a minute's rest. Brer Rabbit longed to see what was happening. He lifted up the teapot lid very cautiously on his long ears and peeped out. And at that very moment Brer Fox saw him!

"Oooooh!" he shouted in fright. "That teapot's got ears! And now it's got eyes! Ooooh, Brer Bear, save me!"

Brer Rabbit giggled so much that he nearly upset the teapot. He stuck his paw out of the spout and waved it to and fro. That made Brer Bear shiver and shake so much that he could hardly stand. Brer Rabbit lifted the lid up and down on his ears, and then jiggled it again. Then he gave a little hop inside the teapot, and the teapot hopped up in the air and down, too! That was too much for Brer Bear and Brer Fox. They fled out of the kitchen as fast as ever they could, shouting "It's after us, it's after us!"

And then old Brer Rabbit climbed out of the big teapot, wiped himself with a tea-cloth, and sat down and laughed till he cried. Oh, Brer Rabbit, how *do* you think of all your pranks and tricks?

Bobs Meets Brer Rabbit Again

ONE FINE MORNING, when Bobs the dog was ambling down the lane, whom should he meet all alive-o but Brer Rabbit. He stopped and stared, and then in a trice he captured him!

"So *you're* the rabbit that eats the cabbages in our garden!" he barked. "Well, you won't eat any more."

"You've made a mistake!" said Brer Rabbit. "That's my brother that eats the cabbages!"

"I don't believe you!" said Bobs, with a growl. "You're the one! You just come along and I'll lock you up in my kennel. Then Sandy and I will ask the mistress to cook you for our dinner."

Poor Brer Rabbit began to shiver and shake. "I tell you, Bobs, you're making a mistake!" he said again. "My brother is exactly like me. You wouldn't like to cook an innocent bunny for your dinner, would you?"

"I shouldn't mind a bit, if he was as fat as you," said Bobs. "I don't believe your tale of a brother, Brer Rabbit! But if we *do* happen to meet a rabbit *exactly* like you, with the *same* number of whiskers and everything, well, I *might* let you go!"

He marched Brer Rabbit up the lane and into the gates of Old Thatch. Soon they came to the little bridge over the stream. When they were in the middle of the bridge Brer Rabbit stopped short and pointed into the water.

"There's my brother!" he said. "Look! Isn't he exactly like me?"

Bobs looked into the water. Sure enough, looking back at him was a bunny just exactly like Brer Rabbit! Bobs counted the whiskers on Brer Rabbit's cheeks, and then he counted those on the rabbit in the water. There were just the same number! As he was counting them the rabbit in the water made a rude face, and Bobs growled angrily.

"Hie, Sandy!" he called. "Come and hold this rabbit while I get the one in the water! Then I'll just see which one it is that steals our cabbages!"

Sandy came running up and took hold of Brer Rabbit. Splash! Bobs jumped into the stream after the rabbit he had seen in there looking up at

him. He growled and spluttered, barked and wuffed—but, dear me, it was very strange, he *couldn't* seem to find that rabbit!

Brer Rabbit looked at Sandy. He was a very little dog. "My!" said Brer Rabbit, "just look at that bone there!"

He pointed downwards to the planks and Sandy bent down to sniff. Brer Rabbit gave him a sharp push, and splash—into the stream went Sandy, right on top of Bobs. Bobs thought he was the rabbit and grabbed hold of him with his teeth. "Shake him, Bobs! Shake him!" yelled Brer Rabbit. "You've got my brother!" So Bobs shook poor Sandy till all his teeth rattled! Then he suddenly saw who it was!

"Goodbye, goodbye, I'll tell my brother I've had such a pleasant morning with you!" giggled Brer Rabbit. "At least I would if I had a brother—but I haven't!"

And off scampered that wicked rabbit in a mighty hurry!

Brer Rabbit's New Shoes

NOW ONCE IT HAPPENED that Brer Rabbit bought himself a pair of new shoes. They were mighty smart ones—black, with red laces—and Brer Rabbit was as pleased with them as a dog with two tails.

He showed them off to all the animals and they got very tired of seeing his new shoes.

"If you got some new manners it would be better," grumbled Brer Fox.

"New shoes are wasted on you," said Brer Wolf. "You should spend your money on a new face. I'm tired of seeing that old one of yours."

These rude remarks didn't upset old Brer Rabbit at all. He just went on wearing his new shoes, showing them off, and being as grand as could be till Brer Fox and Brer Wolf longed to get hold of him and spank him.

"Let's lie in wait for him," said Brer Fox. "I'm just about tired of seeing those new shoes of his. Let's lie in wait for him, pounce on him, take his new shoes, and throw them into the very middle of the pond!"

"That's a fine idea!" said Brer Wolf, pleased. "Brer Rabbit goes to market tomorrow. Let's hide somewhere in the bushes when he comes back. Then we'll jump out on him and give him the fright of his life—and he'll have to say good-bye to his new shoes."

So when Brer Rabbit came whistling back from market next day, Brer Fox and Brer Wolf waited for him. Brer Rabbit had on his new shoes, of course—but he wasn't quite so pleased with them as everybody thought. They hurt him!

"They're just a bit too small," thought Brer Rabbit sadly.

"I should have got a size larger. Now what a pity that is! I can't afford to buy another pair. And I think I'd rather have had a yellow pair with green laces. But still, it's too late now. I must just go on wearing them, and letting them hurt me."

He was thinking all this when he got to the top of the hill that looked down on the wood where he lived. And flying above the wood he saw old Turkey Buzzard, looking down on the trees as if he saw something interesting there.

Brer Rabbit called to him. "Heyo, Brer Buzzard, what's up down there in the wood? Looks like you're watching something."

"So I am, Brer Rabbit, so I am," said Brer Buzzard, sailing over to Brer Rabbit on his big wings. "I can see those two rogues, Brer Fox and Brer Wolf—and it looks to me as if they're lying in wait for somebody. So it does."

"Is that so?" said Brer Rabbit, thinking mighty quickly. "Well, there's only one person coming along this way today, and that's me. So it doesn't need much puzzling to know who's the man they're waiting for! Brer Turkey Buzzard, I'm a-going to hide myself in this bush, and it will take Brer Fox and Brer Wolf a month of Sundays to find me!"

With that Brer Rabbit skipped into the bush nearby, stuck his feet well out at the bottom, and waited to see what Brer Turkey Buzzard would say.

"Your feet show, with your new shoes on," said Brer Turkey Buzzard at once.

"Can't help that," said Brer Rabbit, grinning a bit to himself. "Now don't you tell where I am, Brer Turkey Buzzard."

Brer Turkey Buzzard sailed off into the air. Soon he came to where Brer Fox and Brer Wolf were hiding, and he called to them.

"If you want that scamp

of a Brer Rabbit, I can tell you where he is. He's hiding himself in a bush at the top of the hill, and you can see where he is because his big feet stick out at the bottom—and he's got those new shoes on."

"Thanks, Brer Turkey Buzzard, you're a friend," said Brer Fox, with a grin. "Brer Rabbit won't have those new shoes on long!"

Brer Fox and Brer Wolf made their way to the top of the hill—and it wasn't long before they saw a bush that made them nudge one another and grin. Sticking out at the bottom were Brer Rabbit's grand new shoes!

"There he is, a-hiding in that bush!" whispered Brer Fox.

But Brer Fox was wrong. Brer Rabbit wasn't in that bush at all! As soon as Brer Turkey Buzzard had sailed off to Brer Fox and Brer Wolf, Brer Rabbit had slipped out of the bush and had taken off his shoes. Then he had stuck his shoes at the bottom of the bush so that it looked exactly as if he were in the bush himself, with his feet sticking out at the bottom.

Then old Brer Rabbit skipped to another bush and squeezed himself right into the middle of it. He waited and he waited—and he didn't have to wait long before up crept Brer Fox and Brer Wolf.

Brer Rabbit put his paw over his mouth to stop himself from laughing out loud when he saw the two nudging one another and pointing to the bush where his shoes were. Brer Fox went to one side of the bush and Brer Wolf went to the other.

"Heyo, Brer Rabbit! "said Brer Fox, speaking to the bush.

There was no answer.

"Now, Brer Rabbit, we know you're in that bush, because your great big feet are sticking out at the bottom," said Brer Fox. "You're so mighty proud of those new shoes of yours that you can't even hide them when you want to! Come on out, and we'll give you a spanking!"

No answer from the bush at all. Brer Rabbit giggled to himself. Brer Fox got angry.

"Now look here, Brer Rabbit, you're a sensible man, aren't you? Well, you don't want us to have to pull you out, do you? You just come out yourself. That bush is prickly and we're not going to tear our clothes to bits, I can tell you!"

Brer Fox got no answer at all. Then Brer Wolf spoke up.

"Brer Rabbit! You're not dumb, are you? If you don't speak up and come out, we'll beat the bush down! Then you'll be sorry!"

Brer Rabbit didn't say a word, but he nearly cracked his sides with trying not to laugh.

"Brer Fox, come on! We'll beat that bush with sticks till we make old Brer Rabbit come jumping out in a hurry," said Brer Wolf in a rage. "He thinks we won't try to drag him out because of the thorns. Well—we'll beat him out! Get a stick and we'll begin."

Now it was a hot day, and beating a bush is hot work. So Brer Fox and Brer Wolf took off their coats and laid them down on the grass. Then they cut themselves big sticks and set to work. My, how they beat that bush!

Smack, slap, bang, smack! Blip, blap, smack!

They made such a noise that they didn't hear Brer Rabbit squeeze out of the bush he was in and go to their coats. They didn't see him pick up their coats and stuff them down a rabbit-hole. They didn't see anything at all except the bush they were beating.

After a bit their arms ached badly and they stopped beating the bush. They stared at one another, panting.

"He must be black and blue by now," said Brer Fox. "Brer Rabbit, come along out! We know you're still there because your feet are sticking out!"

Then Brer Wolf looked round for his coat. He meant to get out his handkerchief and mop his face. But his coat wasn't there. He stared round in surprise.

"What have you done with my coat, Brer Fox?" he asked.

"Nothing," said Brer Fox, looking round too. "Where's my coat?"

"They've both gone," said Brer Wolf, puzzled. "Who's taken them?"

"Well, if Brer Rabbit wasn't in this bush I'd think he'd played one of his tricks!" said Brer Fox in a temper. "That's what I think, Brer Wolf!"

Brer Wolf stared at the bush they had been beating. An idea came into his head. He suddenly bent down and snatched at the shoes sticking out at the bottom. They came away in his hand!

"Look there!" he cried. "No feet in them! Brer Rabbit stuck them there to make us think he was in the bush! He's taken our coats, that's what he's done!"

"Well, we'll take his shoes," yelled Brer Fox, and he picked them up. He threw them high into the air and they landed in a tree. The little Jack Sparrows flew away in a fright.

"Brer Rabbit won't wear *those* shoes again!" said Brer Fox. He'll have to wear his old ones—and serve him right too!"

But he didn't! He came out next day in a marvellous pair of new yellow shoes with green laces, and he paraded up and down, showing them off till everyone was wild with him.

"I didn't like the others," he said. "They were too small. So I got Brer Fox to throw them away in the trees and I bought myself a better pair."

"How did you get the money?" asked Brer Terrapin, in surprise. Brer Fox and Brer Wolf listened in a rage.

"Well, you see, Brer Fox and Brer Wolf are just the kindest friends to me," said Brer Rabbit, with a grin. "They gave me their coats—and I exchanged them for this pair of shoes. My, you should see how fast I can run in them!"

And he did too—far too fast for Brer Fox and Brer Wolf to catch him!

Brer Wolf and Brer Fox

ONE DAY BRER WOLF and Brer Fox began to quarrel with one another. It all happened because Brer Rabbit met them, yelled out "Howdy!" and disappeared into a briar-bush before either Brer Wolf or Brer Fox could get him.

"There goes the man that's tricked you more often than you can count!" said Brer Wolf to Brer Fox.

"And he hasn't tricked you, I suppose!" said Brer Fox, in a disagreeable sort of voice. "Oh, no, I suppose he hasn't tricked you, Brer Wolf! What a short memory you've got. Now just let me remind you of a few things—do you remember when Brer Rabbit ..."

"I don't remember anything," said Brer Wolf. "I don't think of Brer Rabbit more than I can help. But I do remember how he frightened you when he was all covered with leaves, shouting out that he was the Wull-of-the-Wust! Ho, you looked scared enough then, Brer Fox!"

"Well," began Brer Fox, in a rage, "and weren't you with me, then? Didn't your whiskers shake as if they were leaves in the wind? Didn't your ears shiver and your tail drop? Lands' sakes, Brer Wolf, you were a lot more scared than I was!"

"Indeed I wasn't," said Brer Wolf, and he began to snap his jaws. Brer Fox snapped his too, and before they had taken two steps they were at one another! Brer Fox lammed out at Brer Wolf and sent him flying. Brer Wolf shot to his feet and snapped his big teeth at Brer Fox. Then Brer Fox sailed in again and hit Brer Wolf on the nose.

Well, Brer Wolf was the bigger of the two, so it wasn't long before Brer Fox knew he'd better be going! So he watched his

chance, and slipped away under Brer Wolf's paws and ran into the wood.

Brer Wolf shot after him, and he ran so fast that he was on Brer Fox's tail all the time. And Brer Fox knew that the only way to save his skin was to hide in a hole somewhere, so the first hollow tree he came to he dived inside!

Brer Wolf made a grab at him, but he was just in time to be too late! Brer Fox was in that hole and in that hole he stayed. It was too small for Brer Wolf to get inside, so Brer Wolf sat outside and thought what he was going to do to get Brer Fox out. And Brer Fox lay in the hole and wondered what Brer Wolf was going to do!

"Well," said Brer Wolf, at last, "seems I can't get Brer Fox out—but I can make him stay in! Oh, yes, I can make him stay in all right! He'll wish he'd never gone inside that tree before long. I'm a-going to get some big chunky stones, and they'll be set in the hole of the tree, and old Brer Fox won't come out again. Oh, no, he won't!"

So Brer Wolf hunted round a bit and got together a big pile of earth, rocks and sticks, and he filled up the hole with them. He knew Brer Fox wouldn't be able to get out, and he chuckled to himself as he lammed the rocks and the sticks into the hole.

Whilst all this was going on Brer Turkey Buzzard flew above, going about his business. He happened to look down and what did he see but old Brer Wolf a-piling up rocks and sticks in the hole of the hollow tree. Brer Turkey Buzzard was quite astonished.

"I'll just sort of flop down and look into this," he said to himself, "because if Brer Wolf is hiding his dinner there expecting to find it when he comes back, then he's gone and put it in the wrong place!"

With that old Brer Turkey Buzzard flopped down and sailed round nearer. Then he flopped down a bit more and sat on the top of the hollow tree. Brer Wolf got a glimpse of Brer Buzzard's shadow but he took no notice. He just went on putting the chunks of wood in the hole.

Presently Brer Turkey Buzzard began to talk to him.

"What are you doing there, Brer Wolf?"

"No business of yours, Brer Buzzard," said Brer Wolf.

"Brer Wolf, if you ever want to buy a little politeness, you come along to me and I'll sell you some," said Brer Buzzard.

"You sell it to Brer Rabbit, Brer Buzzard, or keep it for yourself," said Brer Wolf. "You could both do with some!"

"I never did like you, Brer Wolf," said Brer Buzzard.

"You be careful what you say to me, Brer Buzzard," said Brer Wolf, snapping his jaws. "If you aren't careful I'll put you in this hollow tree with Brer Fox!"

"Hoo!" said Brer Buzzard, flapping his big wings, "you don't mean to tell me you've got Brer Fox in that tree, Brer

59

Wolf! You're just telling me that because you don't want me to go looking for your dinner there, or your gold, that you're hiding!"

Brer Wolf didn't say another word. He kept on piling up the hole till it was properly stopped up, and then he brushed the dust off his clothes and set out for home. Old Brer Turkey

Buzzard, he sat up at the top of the tree and listened and listened, and untangled his tail-feathers, but he couldn't hear a thing inside the tree. Brer Fox lay low and kept quiet, so there wasn't anything for Brer Buzzard to hear.

After a while Brer Buzzard sailed round in the air again, and this time he sang, and this is the song he sang:

"Boo, boo, boo, my filler-me-loo,
There's a man out here with
news for you!"

Now when one of the creatures sang this, anyone that heard it would answer at once. But Brer Fox, he didn't answer a word. He just lay low and kept quiet. Brer Buzzard flopped down to the tree again, and put his head on one side and listened with both his ears. But he couldn't hear a thing.

"This is mighty funny," he thought to himself. "If Brer Fox was inside, he'd answer me all right. But he doesn't answer, so maybe he isn't there—and if he isn't there, then nobody else is—and it must be Brer Wolf's dinner there, or maybe his gold! Well, I'll wait a while and then I'll sail around again and sing."

So he sat on the tree and waited. Then after a time he sailed into the air and sang his song.

> *"Boo, boo, boo, my filler-me-loo,*
> *There's a man out here with news for you!"*

He flopped down on the tree and listened hard. But not a sound did he hear. Brer Fox, he lay low inside the tree.

"This is where I get right down and find Brer Wolf's dinner!" said old Brer Turkey Buzzard to himself. So down he sailed to the ground and cocked his head at the pile of stones and sticks round about the hole.

He took one chunk out and listened. Not a sound came from the hole. He took another chunk out and listened. No, not a sound from the hole. Brer Fox lay as low as he could, listening to Brer Buzzard uncovering the hole.

Brer Buzzard went on taking away the wood and the earth and the stones. Soon Brer Fox could see daylight—and when he saw fat old Brer Buzzard there his mouth began to water too! Brer Buzzard worked on, taking chunks and sticks away, singing a little song in between whiles, and keeping a sharp look-out for Brer Wolf in case he came back.

When the hole was almost uncovered Brer Buzzard sniffed to see if he could smell the dinner he thought might be inside the hole. But he couldn't smell dinner—and yet he could smell something! It couldn't be gold—gold didn't smell. Then what could it be?

"Tails and feathers, Brer Wolf was telling me the truth—it's Brer Fox in there!" Brer Buzzard screeched suddenly. And he rose up into the air just as Brer Fox shot out of the hole and made a grab at him. Brer Fox caught three of his tail-feathers, but that was all. Brer Buzzard sailed away high in the air, and Brer Fox sat outside that hole, holding the feathers in his hand and looking as disappointed as three wet Saturdays!

"Is that the way to treat a friend!" screeched Brer Buzzard in a rage. "Didn't I set you free? I'm off to tell Brer Wolf you're out of the hole!"

Brer Fox didn't wait to hear any more. He raced through the wood, lippitty, clippitty, and didn't stop till he was safe indoors with all the windows and doors bolted!

Brer Rabbit and Mr. Man

IT HAPPENED ONE DAY that Brer Rabbit met Brer Fox, and they asked each other, "Howdy?"

"Howdy, Brer Fox?" said Brer Rabbit. "I hope you're feeling well."

"Howdy, Brer Rabbit?" said Brer Fox. "Thank you kindly, but I'm feeling poorly."

"Is that so?" said Brer Rabbit. "Then we'd better go along together, Brer Fox, for I'm feeling mighty poorly too."

"I'm so hungry I could eat grass," said Brer Fox.

"I'm mighty hungry too," said Brer Rabbit. "But I want something more than grass. Look, Brer Fox, who's this a-coming down the road?"

"It's Mr. Man," said Brer Fox. "And what's that he's got over his shoulder, Brer Rabbit?"

"It's a great big hunk of beef!" said Brer Rabbit.

"I'd like mighty well to get a taste of that beef," said Brer Fox.

Well, Mr. Man came along, and Brer Fox and Brer Rabbit looked and looked at him and the meat. They winked at one another.

"I've just got to get that meat!" said Brer Rabbit.

"It looks mighty far off to me," said Brer Fox.

"Now just you listen to me, Brer Fox," said Brer Rabbit. "You follow along behind me a good way off, and watch what I do. I've got a mighty fine plan!"

And with that Brer Rabbit set off and soon caught up with Mr. Man.

"Howdy, Mr. Man?" said Brer Rabbit.

"Howdy, Brer Rabbit?" said Mr. Man. "Fine day, this."

"It is that," said Brer Rabbit. And then they went on together, chatting away like old friends.

Brer Rabbit kept on sniffing the air—sniff-sniff-sniff.

"Have you got a bad cold?" asked Mr. Man.

"No, Mr. Man," said Brer Rabbit. "I haven't got a cold—I'm only smelling something—and it doesn't smell to me like ripe peaches either! No, that it doesn't!"

"Well, I can't smell anything wrong," said Mr. Man. Pretty soon Brer Rabbit began to hold his nose and pretend to feel sick. After a while he shouted out to Mr. Man.

"Gracious goodness, Mr. Man! It's that meat of yours that is smelling so bad! Wherever did you pick up that meat?"

This made Mr. Man feel sort of ashamed of himself, to be carrying bad meat home. He thought it was mighty strange that he couldn't smell it was bad—and no wonder either, for that meat was as fresh as a new-laid egg! There was nothing bad about it at all—it was just Brer Rabbit's wicked trick.

Brer Rabbit went to the other side of the road, and held his nose for all he was worth. Mr. Man looked sorry, and before they had gone much farther he put the meat down on the side of the road.

"What shall I do about it?" he said. "It can't be very bad—but if it smells like you say I'll have to do something about it before I take it home."

"Well," said Brer Rabbit, looking wise, "I did once hear tell that if you take and drag a piece of meat through the dust it will make it fresh and good again. I've never tried it myself, mind you, but those that have done it tell me it comes all right again. And, anyway, it can't do any harm to the meat, because you can always wash the dust off!"

"I haven't got any string to pull it along in the dust," said Mr. Man.

Brer Rabbit laughed loudly, but he still held his nose.

"If you'd lived in the woods as long as I have, you wouldn't be without strings!" he said.

And with that Brer Rabbit hopped into the bushes, and soon came back with a long string of bamboo vines tied together to make a good strong rope.

"That's a mighty long string," said Mr. Man.

"To be sure it is!" said Brer Rabbit. "But if you have a short string, you're going to smell that meat, Mr. Man, and you don't want to do that. It's a dreadful smell, sure enough!"

Then Mr. Man tied his piece of meat on to the end of the bamboo rope.

Brer Rabbit broke a branch off an elder bush and said he would stay behind with the meat and brush the flies off it, as Mr. Man pulled it along. So Mr. Man, he went on in front and dragged the meat, and Brer Rabbit stayed behind, he did, to take care of it!

And he did take care of it, too! He got a rock, undid the meat, and tied the rock on to the string instead! Mr. Man went on in front, pulling the rope without looking back—and when Brer Fox came on behind, there, sure enough, was the hunk of meat lying by itself in the road—and on ahead was Brer Rabbit pretending to brush flies off the large rock! Mr. Man he went on in front, dragging and pulling.

After a while Mr. Man looked back to see what Brer Rabbit was doing, and to ask him if the meat was smelling better—but where was old Brer Rabbit?

He had run back to join Brer Fox—and he was just in time, too, because in another minute Brer Fox would have gobbled up all that meat, and that would have been the end of it!

And that's the way Brer Rabbit got Mr. Man's meat. Ah—but wait a minute: who's going to eat it—Brer Fox, or Brer Rabbit?

How Brer Rabbit Got the Meat

WELL, AFTER BRER RABBIT got the meat from Mr. Man, and rushed back to Brer Fox—*terbuckity-buckity, buck-buck-buckity*—they carried the meat a good way off in the woods, and laid it down on a clean piece of ground.

"We'd better taste it," said Brer Fox.

"That's so," said Brer Rabbit.

So Brer Fox gnawed off a big hunk, shut both eyes and chewed and chewed and tasted and tasted, and chewed and tasted. Brer Rabbit watched him, and then he started on the meat too.

Brer Fox smacked his lips, looked closely at the meat, and said: "Brer Rabbit, it's lamb!"

"No, Brer Fox, surely not!"

"Brer Rabbit, it's lamb!"

"Brer Fox, to be sure not!"

Then Brer Rabbit gnawed off a chunk, shut both eyes, and chewed and tasted and tasted and chewed. Then he smacked his lips and said: "Brer Fox, it's pork!"

"Brer Rabbit, it's not!"

"Brer Fox, I vow it's pork!"

"Brer Rabbit, it just can't be!"

"Brer Fox, it surely is!"

Well, they tasted and they argued and they argued and they tasted. After a while Brer Rabbit said he wanted some water, because pork always made him thirsty, and he rushed off into the bushes. He came back wiping his mouth and clearing his throat as if he had just been drinking—but he hadn't really.

Well, as soon as Brer Fox saw Brer Rabbit wiping his mouth, he felt thirsty, and he spoke to Brer Rabbit.

"Brer Rabbit, where did you find the water?"

"Across the road, and down the hill, and up the big gully," said Brer Rabbit, at once.

Well, Brer Fox, he loped off, he did, and after he had gone Brer Rabbit waved his paw to him in a cheeky manner, and grinned all across his face. Brer Fox crossed the road, rushed down the hill—but he couldn't find any gully. He kept on till he found a gully at last—but there wasn't any water there!

Whilst Brer Fox was gone, Brer Rabbit dug a hole in the ground and hid the meat there. After he had hidden it well he went to a tree and cut a long hickory stick. Then he sat down and waited for Brer Fox to come back.

Very soon he heard him. Then Brer Rabbit got into a clump of bushes, and took the hickory stick with him. There was a young tree near by, and Brer Rabbit began to hit it with his hickory stick as hard as ever he could. And every time he hit the tree Brer Rabbit squealed out as if Mr. Man had got him and was beating him hard!

Pow-pow-pow!

"Oh, mercy, Mr. Man!"

Pow-wow!

"Oh, please, Mr. Man!"

Chippy-row, pow!

"Oh, Mr. Man, let me go! Brer Fox took your meat!"

Pow-pow-pow!

Well, when Brer Fox heard all this noise going on—*pow-pow-pow*, as if Brer Rabbit was being well whipped—and then

Brer Rabbit squealing, he stopped in a hurry and listened hard.

And every time Brer Fox heard that hickory stick coming down *pow*, he grinned to himself.

"Ah-yi, Brer Rabbit! You tricked me about that water, didn't you! And now Mr. Man's got you! Ah-yi!"

Well, after some time, the noise stopped, and Brer Fox listened to see what was going to happen next; and he heard a noise as if Brer Rabbit was being dragged off by Mr. Man— but it was really old Brer Rabbit dragging a big branch through the bushes, and grinning from ear to ear! Brer Fox listened to this, and he felt mighty pleased.

"Ho! Mr. Man's dragging Brer Rabbit off by his hind legs! Ah-yi! You tricked me about that water, Brer Rabbit! Now you're getting punished for it! Ah-yi!"

By and by Brer Rabbit came tearing through the woods as if he'd escaped from Mr. Man. He was shouting at the top of his voice.

"Run, Brer Fox, run! Mr. Man says he's going to take the meat up the road to where his son is—and then he's coming back after *you*, Brer Fox! He's cut a new hickory stick to beat you. Run, Brer Fox, run!"

Brer Fox flicked up his heels and ran as if the dogs were after him—and old Brer Rabbit, he sat down by the hole where he had hidden his meat, and he dug it up and ate it in peace. And when he thought of Brer Fox running away from it, he just laughed and danced and kicked up his feet like mad. There never was such a rascal as old Brer Rabbit.

Brer Fox Has a Surprise

ONCE UPON A TIME Brer Rabbit wanted to play a trick on Brer Fox. He took Brer Terrapin into his secret, and the two of them made a plan, with many grins and giggles.

Brer Rabbit fetched a sack, and propped the mouth open with a stick. Inside he put a fish he had caught the day before. It smelt rather strong, but that was how he wanted it to smell.

"Now we'll get into the hedge and wait for Cousin Wildcat to come along," he said.

So the two of them crept into the hedge and lay low. Presently along came Cousin Wildcat, hissing between his teeth, and kicking the dead leaves with his feet.

When he came near the sack he smelt the fish. He stopped at once and sniffed.

"I smell fish!" he said. "Good fish—a day old!"

Brer Rabbit nudged Brer Terrapin and the two of them tried their hardest not to laugh.

Cousin Wildcat sniffed again. Then he saw the sack with its neck propped open, and he was rather astonished. He went nearer to see what it was—and the smell of the fish came strongly from out of the sack.

"The fish is in there!" said Cousin Wildcat, and looked around to see who the sack belonged to. But he could see nobody.

"Funny!" he said. "Very funny! I suppose somebody is fishing somewhere and they are putting their fish into this sack. But why leave the sack alone? Somebody might take the fish. In fact, I think I had better take it myself in case someone comes along and gets it."

So in the sack went Cousin Wildcat after that fish. And as soon as he was well in the sack Brer Rabbit ran out of the hedge, pulled the string that ran round the neck of the sack, and there was Cousin Wildcat nicely caught inside!

My, how he wriggled and struggled! How he yowled and bit and scratched at that sack! But he couldn't get out, for the sack was well and truly tied at the neck by old Brer Rabbit!

"We'll let him struggle till he's tired out," whispered Brer Rabbit. "Then you can go and fetch Brer Fox and say exactly what we've planned for you to say."

So they let poor Cousin Wildcat wriggle and fight and struggle inside the sack till he was too tired to do it any more. When he was lying still, Brer Rabbit winked at Brer Terrapin and Brer Terrapin began to lumber away to Brer Fox's house, which was quite nearby.

When he got there he saw Brer Fox in the garden, digging. "Heyo, Brer Fox!" cried Brer Terrapin. "Will you come and help me, please?"

"What's the matter?" asked Brer Fox.

"I've found somebody tied up in a sack in the woods," said Brer Terrapin. "And it might be Brer Rabbit, you know. Could you come and undo the sack? My great clawed feet won't undo knots."

"Oh, I'll certainly come along," said Brer Fox at once, feeling sure that it

must be Brer Rabbit in the sack, for he knew that Brer Terrapin was Brer Rabbit's friend. "I'll certainly come along. It will be a great pleasure, Brer Terrapin."

Brer Fox meant to carry Brer Rabbit home in that sack! That certainly *would* be a great pleasure! Aha, he would have that scamp of a rabbit in his power for once!

Brer Terrapin grinned to himself. He took Brer Fox to the woods and they came to the sack. Cousin Wildcat was lying quiet. Brer Rabbit was well hidden in the hedge.

"There's the sack," said Brer Terrapin. "It may not be Brer Rabbit in it, Brer Fox, so look out when you undo the string."

"I think I'll undo the sack when I get home," said Brer Fox, and he jerked the sack up to his shoulder. That stirred up Cousin Wildcat and he began to yowl like a railway engine letting off steam.

"Never heard Brer Rabbit make *that* noise before," said Brer Fox to Brer Terrapin. "He must be mighty frightened ! Ow!"

Brer Fox yelled out "Ow!" because Cousin Wildcat had just dug a very sharp claw into his shoulder. He dug another one in, and Brer Fox grew angry.

"You wait till I get you out of this sack, Brer Rabbit!" he shouted. "I'll empty you into a pan of water on my stove and you'll cook there for my dinner!"

Cousin Wildcat went quite mad in the sack. He wriggled and fought till Brer Fox could hardly hold the sack on his shoulder, and at last he let it drag along the ground. This bumped Cousin Wildcat dreadfully, and he grew even madder.

Brer Terrapin went along with Brer Fox, and Brer Rabbit skipped behind the hedge, watching. Brer Fox went into his house and put a big pan of water on to the stove. Then he pulled open the string round the neck of the sack—and out fell Cousin Wildcat into the water!

Well, all cats, wild or tame, hate water, and Cousin Wildcat hated it more than most. He leapt out of that pan as soon as he was in it—and he flew at poor Brer Fox like a Spitfire! My, how he spat and hissed and bit and scratched! Brer Fox shut his eyes and fought for all he was worth—and at last Cousin Wildcat jumped out of the window and disappeared into the woods with a yowl! Brer Fox quite thought it had been Brer Rabbit all the time, and he sat down in a chair and got his breath back, feeling very puzzled indeed to think of Brer Rabbit's suddenly sharp claws.

Brer Rabbit peeped in at the door, grinning all over his face. "Like another fight with me, Brer Fox?" he asked, and he put up his two small fists. "Come along! It was good of you to let me out of the sack—but you couldn't expect me to like the pan of water! Come along—let's have another fight!"

But Brer Fox had had such a shock that he wasn't going to fight with anybody in the world, not even with old Brer Terrapin who was laughing fit to crack his shell. He got up and banged his door.

"Tell me when you want a fight, Brer Fox, and I'll come and give you one!" shouted Brer Rabbit, as he went off with Brer Terrapin. But he didn't hear a word from Brer Fox for many a long day.

Brer Rabbit and the Flower Pot

ONCE MISS BEAR said to Brer Bear, "Brer Bear, I want to cook some onions for dinner. You go and get some out of the shed."

Brer Bear's onions were stored in his shed, big and round and shiny. Brer Bear went to get some.

He got eight large onions and went back to Miss Bear. "Now you just sit out there in the garden and peel them for me," she said. "They make my eyes water, but maybe yours won't."

So Brer Bear sat on the garden seat in the sun, and began to peel the onions. And who should come by at that very moment but old Brer Rabbit. He sniffed the smell of onions at once. My, it was good!

"Heyo, Brer Bear!" said Brer Rabbit, peeping over the fence. "Those are fine onions you've got. You might spare me a little one for my supper tonight."

"Brer Rabbit, I'm sparing you nothing, unless you'd like the peel," said Brer Bear. "And don't you think you can steal any, because you can't. I'm sitting here by my onions till they're finished—and if you think you can get even the smallest one, well, you're welcome to try. But you'll get my hand at the back of your neck too!"

"Brer Bear, keep your smelly old onions," said Brer Rabbit in a huff. "I'm off to get a lift to the market, and I'll buy better onions there than any of yours!"

Off he went, and Brer Bear grinned to himself. "He won't find better onions than these, and he knows it!" he said. "He'll have to spend all day looking round the market for onions as big as these!"

But Brer Rabbit hadn't gone to market. No—he was just the other side of the hedge, watching to see if Brer Bear would leave his onions for a minute. Hadn't Brer Bear said he could have one if he could get one? All right—Brer Rabbit guessed he *would* get one.

But Brer Bear didn't leave his onions at all until he wanted to blow his nose. And then he didn't go indoors to get his hanky. He went to the kitchen window and yelled.

"Miss Bear—hey, Miss Bear! Pass me out my red hanky!"

While his back was turned for that second, Brer Rabbit hopped in at the gate, went to a big red flower pot that stood upside down nearby, and popped himself under it. The pot covered him up completely. Brer Bear got his red hanky and went back to his seat to peel his onions.

Pretty soon Brer Rabbit moved a little nearer to Brer Bear, but nothing could be seen except that the flower pot slid along a little way. Brer Bear didn't notice it.

Brer Rabbit slid a little nearer and then a little nearer still. Still Brer Bear didn't notice. He went on peeling the onions, wiping the tears from his eyes every now and again.

At last Brer Rabbit was so near the onions that he could smell them. He waited until he heard old Brer Bear sneeze—and then, quick as lightning, Brer Rabbit put a paw out from under the

pot, took hold of an onion, pulled it back under the pot, and stayed quite still.

"A-TISH-OO!" said Brer Bear and sneezed into his hanky. Then he reached down to the ground for the last onion.

But it wasn't there! Brer Bear looked all round him, quite surprised. The onion had been there the minute before. Well, then, it should be there now. But it wasn't.

"Most peculiar," said Brer Bear, and he felt about in the bits of brown that had come from the outside of the onions. But the onion wasn't there either.

Then Brer Bear noticed something that made him feel rather queer. A large flower pot nearby moved off a little. Brer Bear stared at it. It kept quite still.

"My eyes must be going wrong," thought Brer Bear, mopping them. "Flower pots don't walk."

But that one did. Even as Brer Bear looked at it again, it moved a little further off, and then stayed still once more.

"Well, now, I never saw a flower pot that walked before!" said Brer Bear, puzzled. "No, that I never did. Things are coming to a queer pass if flower pots begin to walk."

Now just then Brer Fox came walking by and he called over the fence. "Heyo, Brer Bear! How's yourself?"

"Brer Fox, I'm feeling mighty queer," said Brer Bear. "I'm seeing flower pots that walk."

"What did you say?" said Brer Fox, thinking he must have heard wrong. Brer Bear told him again. Brer Fox came in at the gate. He looked round at the flower pots in the garden. There were three or four there, as well as the one that Brer Rabbit was hiding under.

"Well, they all seem to be staying quite still," said Brer Fox. "Your eyes must be wrong."

"Yes, I think they must be," said poor Brer Bear. "Maybe I ought to wear glasses. See—that's the one that keeps moving, Brer Fox. That one there."

He pointed—and Brer Fox stared as if his eyes would drop out of his head. Certainly that flower pot was moving! It was moving towards the gate.

"Stars and moon!" said Brer Fox, feeling a bit scared. "That's an odd thing. Does it just walk like that, Brer Bear—it doesn't do anything else, does it? Because if it does, I'm going. I don't like things like that."

Well, when old Brer Rabbit heard what Brer Fox said, he grinned to himself. All right—if Brer Fox was going to be scared, Brer Rabbit would scare him properly! So old Brer Rabbit began to jig up and down inside the pot, and he made it dance like mad.

Brer Fox clutched hold of Brer Bear in fright, and the two of them shivered and shook.

"It's dancing now!" said Brer Bear in a shaking voice.

And then that pot began to sing! Of course, it was just old Brer Rabbit singing away in a funny deep voice under the pot, but it sounded mighty queer, all the same.

> *"There isn't a pot in the world like me,*
> *I'm just as mad as a pot can be,*
> *Hi-tiddle-hi, and ho-tiddle-ho,*
> *I'll dance on my heel and I'll dance on my toe!"*

79

Then the pot went quite mad, and rushed round in circles, jiggled and jerked, and made terrible screeching noises till Brer Bear and Brer Fox almost fell over in fright.

Miss Bear came out to see what the matter was. "Lawks!" she cried, "look at that! Oh my, oh my, what's going to happen next?"

Well, what happened next, happened all in a hurry. The pot danced to the gate and went through it. It disappeared behind the hedge—and as soon as it was out of sight Brer Rabbit popped out from under it, scurried into the hedge with his onion, and laughed fit to kill himself.

After a bit Brer Bear, Miss Bear, and Brer Fox tiptoed to the gate and looked down the lane. And there they saw the pot, tipped on its side, quite still. They stared at one another. More and more peculiar!

Then a bit of brown onion-peel flew into the roadway by their feet, and a cheeky voice cried out:

> "Hi-tiddle-hi! and ho-tiddle-ho,
> I'll dance on my heel and I'll dance on my toe!"

And down the road, as quick as could be, danced old Brer Rabbit, first on his heels, and then on his toes, munching away at the onion as he went. Brer Bear gave a bellow and went after him—but Brer Rabbit was mighty quick and went down a hole before Brer Bear could so much as touch his tail!

"He got that onion after all!" said Brer Bear. "My, he's a scamp if ever there was one. Now I wonder how he got it?"

But none of the three could guess. As for the flower pot, Brer Bear threw a stone at it and broke it.

"I'm not going to have you dancing and singing at me any more!" he said. And didn't old Brer Rabbit laugh when he heard that!

Brer Fox is Much Too Smart

ONE DAY BRER FOX remembered how Brer Rabbit had tricked him by lying down in front of him pretending to be dead. And Brer Fox thought it was a mighty good idea.

"Seems like I might trick Mr. Man if I did the same," said Brer Fox to himself. "Suppose I did that when Mr. Man was going along to the market with his chickens and ducks and other goods. Maybe Mr. Man would leave his goods and go back and collect the dead foxes he thought he'd seen—and I could make off with a nice meal!"

So Brer Fox kept watching for a chance to play the same kind of game. By and by he heard Mr. Man coming down the high road in a one-horse wagon, carrying some chickens, some eggs, and some butter to market.

Brer Fox heard him coming, he did, and what did he do but go and lie down in the road in front of the wagon! Mr. Man, he drove along, clucking to the horse and humming to himself, and when they had almost got up to Brer Fox the horse shied. Mr. Man was surprised.

"Wo there!" he cried. And the horse woed. Then Mr. Man looked down to see why his horse had shied, and he saw Brer Fox lying out there on the ground just as if he was dead.

"Heyo!" he shouted. "There's the chap that's been stealing my chickens! Somebody's shot him with a gun—and I wish it had been two guns, so I do!"

With that Mr. Man drove on and left Brer Fox lying there. Then Brer Fox got up and ran round through the woods and lay down in front of Mr. Man again. Mr. Man came driving along and he saw Brer Fox and said: "Heyo! Here's the chap that has

been killing my pigs! Somebody's killed *him*, and I wish they'd done it a long time ago!"

Then Mr. Man, he drove on, and the wagon-wheel came mighty near to running over Brer Fox's nose. But all the same Brer Fox leapt up and ran round ahead of Mr. Man and lay down in the road once more. And when Mr. Man drove up again, there he was all stretched out, big enough to fill a two-bushel basket, looking as dead as could be.

Mr. Man drove up and stopped. He looked down on Brer Fox in surprise, because he thought this was the third dead fox he had seen that morning. Then he looked all round to see if he could spy what it was that was killing so many foxes! But he didn't see anything and he didn't hear anything either.

Then he sat and thought, and by and by he said to himself he'd better get down and have a look at the fox, and see if there was some curious kind of illness that was killing off all the foxes in the wood.

So he got down from the wagon and pulled at Brer Fox's ear. It was quite warm and soft. He felt Brer Fox's neck. It was as warm as his ear. Then he poked Brer Fox in the ribs. No bones seemed to be broken. Then he felt Brer Fox's legs, but they were all as sound as could be. Then he turned Brer Fox over and there didn't seem to be a thing the matter with him at all.

When Mr. Man saw this, he was astonished.

"Heyo, there! What does this mean?" he said to himself. "This chicken-stealer looks as if he's dead, but he hasn't got any broken bones, and he isn't cut or bruised! He feels warm and alive. Something's wrong here, for sure!"

Mr. Man scratched his head and looked down at Brer Fox. He thought of the other two dead foxes he had seen that day, and he thought of all the chickens, eggs and butter in his cart.

"This pig-stealer *might* be dead, and then again he mightn't!" said Mr. Man. "Before I go back and get those other foxes, I'll just make sure."

He caught up his whip. "To make sure he's not alive I'll just give him a whack with my whip-handle," said Mr. Man. And with that Mr. Man lifted up his whip and hit Brer Fox a clip behind the ears—*pow!*—and the blow came so quick and so hard that Brer Fox really thought he had been killed!

But before Mr. Man could lift up the whip again and give him another clip, Brer Fox scrambled to his feet, and ran for his life through the woods!

He was alive all right—and that's all Brer Fox got for playing Mr. Smarty and copying old Brer Rabbit!

Good for You, Brer Rabbit

ONCE BRER FOX and Brer Wolf found a key in the road. They picked it up and looked at it—and then they winked at one another.

"Ho! This is Brer Rabbit's front door key! Now, isn't that a bit of luck!"

"We'll be able to unlock his door and hide in his kitchen," said Brer Wolf.

"And pounce out at him when he comes in!" said Brer Fox.

"We'll do it this very day!" said Brer Wolf.

So the two of them went right off to Brer Rabbit's house, and unlocked his door. They knew he had gone to market, because it was Thursday, and he always went on that day.

They shut the door again, and looked round the kitchen "Where shall we hide?" said Brer Fox.

"I'll go into that cupboard, where the brooms and brushes are kept," said Brer Wolf. And in he went, squeezing his big body between broom-handles and mops.

"I'm going into this cupboard under the dresser," said Brer Fox. "There are a whole lot of pans and dishes here, but I think I can manage to squeeze inside."

The two of them lay in their cupboards as quiet as mice, waiting and waiting for Brer Rabbit to come home from market. They got rather stiff, but they didn't dare to move in case Brer Rabbit happened to come in just at that moment.

Pretty soon along came Brer Rabbit, all hung about with his marketing. He had cabbages and butter, a tin of pepper and a tin of salt, a jar of honey, a pot of jam, six new-laid eggs, and a lot of other things besides. He set them down to get his key out of his pocket.

Brer Fox and Brer Wolf heard him coming. "Now don't you make a sound, Brer Fox!" hissed Brer Wolf from the broom cupboard.

"Well, don't you either!" whispered Brer Fox.

Brer Rabbit couldn't find his key in his pocket. He hunted first in this one and then in that one. "Surely I haven't lost it!" he groaned. "I did hear something drop on my way to market. Oh my, I do hope I haven't lost it."

Well, of course, he *had* lost it, so he didn't find it in his pockets. In despair he tried the handle of his door—and it opened! Brer Rabbit stared at it in surprise.

"Well, didn't I lock the door behind me this morning when I left?" he said to himself. "I always do. This is mighty funny."

He took a look round—and there in the dust outside the front gate he saw the footmarks of Brer Fox and Brer Wolf, as plain as could be!

"Oho!" said Brer Rabbit to himself, scratching his ears and thinking hard. "Oho! And aha! This is where old Brer Rabbit does a bit of thinking!"

He rubbed his nose, and felt certain that Brer Fox and Brer Wolf had picked up his key, and come along and used it on his door! That's why the door wasn't locked now. They were hiding inside—and hoped that he would come and skip indoors as usual. Then what a commotion there would be!

"This won't do," said Brer Rabbit. "This just won't do! I've got to get them out of there somehow—and I can't go in myself, because if I do they'll get me!"

He sat down on his parcels and packets—and a tin rolled out from them. It was the tin of pepper. Brer Rabbit picked it up and grinned. Pepper! That was just the thing!

Brer Fox and Brer Wolf were peeping out of the key-holes in the cupboards, watching and waiting for Brer Rabbit to come in. They were shivering with excitement, for Brer Rabbit looked as fat as butter that day.

Brer Rabbit took the tin of pepper and went to the open door. He cautiously put his paw round and shook the tin with all his might. Shake, shake, shake! Shake, shake, shake, shake! My goodness, you should have seen the pepper fly out of that tin! It flew up to the ceiling. It flew down to the floor. It flew to the other side of the room and back again. It went in at the cracks and key-holes of the cupboards—and it found its way to the eyes and noses of Brer Fox and Brer Wolf!

Brer Wolf felt a sneeze coming. It came nearer and nearer to his nose. He tried his hardest to stop it. He put his paws to his mouth and nose and stopped breathing, hoping that the sneeze wouldn't come.

And when it came it was a MONSTER sneeze. "A-TISH-ISH-OOO!"

Two brooms fell down and a mop fell sideways, knocking Brer Wolf on the nose. Brer Fox called out angrily, in a loud whisper:

"Brer Wolf! Must you make a noise like that just when Brer Rabbit is around?"

And then the pepper got into Brer Fox's nose and eyes, too. He screwed up his face. He tried to squash the sneeze into his throat and not let it come. But it did come.

"Woosh, WOOSH!" sneezed Brer Fox, and then he coughed as if he had whooping-cough, for the pepper was as strong as could be. He just couldn't stop. He coughed a saucepan down on

top of him. He coughed two dishes from the shelf above and they flattened both his ears. Then he sneezed again so loudly that a saucepan fell right on his head like a hat.

"Brer Fox! What do you think you're doing?" said Brer Wolf in a rage. "You tell *me* not to make a noise—but you sound like a thunderstorm and an earthquake all in one!"

Brer Rabbit giggled to himself. Then he spoke in a loud voice, as if he were very puzzled.

"Dear me! What's all that noise in my kitchen, I wonder? I don't like it. No, indeed I don't. It sounds as if robbers and thieves are there, stealing my brooms and my saucepans. I'm going to get Mr. Dog, and ask him to sniff around and hunt out those robbers. An, Mr. Dog has big, sharp teeth and a dreadful bite—*he'll* soon sniff them out!"

Then Brer Rabbit made a pattering noise with his feet as if he were running down the path to fetch Mr. Dog. He crouched down behind a bush and waited.

Now, when Brer Fox and Brer Wolf heard Brer Rabbit talking about Mr. Dog they shivered and shook, for if there was one person they were really afraid of, it was sharp Mr. Dog. He had chased them many a time. Brer Wolf spoke from the broom cupboard.

"Brer Fox! Isn't it time we went? I don't mind waiting about for Brer Rabbit—but I'm not waiting for Mr. Dog!"

"Nor am I!" said Brer Fox, with a mighty sneeze, and he got out of the pan cupboard. "Goodness me, we must both have got terrible colds, the way we're sneezing and coughing. We'd better go home and get into bed with hot-water bottles. I never knew a cold come on so suddenly!"

Brer Rabbit gave a bark like a dog. Brer Wolf and Brer Fox jumped, and made for the door as fast as they could. They got there at the same moment, and stuck.

"Let me out first!" panted Brer Fox, and he hit Brer Wolf with his fist. Brer Wolf gave him a punch back, and Brer Rabbit almost killed himself with laughing to see them.

Then down the path they went at top speed, Brer Fox still with a saucepan on his head that slipped down over his eyes so that he couldn't see where he was going.

"Yap-yap-yap!" barked Brer Rabbit, and the two of them went faster than ever. Everyone thought they must be running a race.

And after that Brer Rabbit had a new lock put on his door. He didn't want any more unexpected visitors!

Mr. Benjamin Ram and his Fiddle

MR. BENJAMIN RAM was a handy man with the fiddle. He lived all by himself out in the middle of the wood, and he was such a fine fellow to have at a dance that all the other creatures liked him very much. When there was any party on they always sent for old man Ram and his fiddle.

And as soon as Mr. Benjamin Ram began to play tunes on his fiddle, why, everyone in the room was up and dancing, shaking their feet and tapping their toes for all they were worth—even old Brer Wolf had to dance when he heard Benjamin Ram's fiddle going.

After the party the other creatures always filled up a bag of peas for old man Ram, and he carried it home with him. He didn't ask anything more than that, for he was a kindly fellow, and liked nothing better than to tune up his fiddle and get people to shake their toes.

One time, just about Christmas, Miss Meadows and the girls thought they would give a party, and they sent word to Mr. Benjamin Ram to come and bring his fiddle. So, when the day came, Mr. Benjamin Ram set out. But the wind blew cold, and the clouds spread so thickly across the sky that it was almost as dark as night.

"No matter!" said Mr. Benjamin Ram. He had his walking-stick with him, and his fiddle tied up in a bag. He knew the way very well, but seeing that it looked so like rain old man Ram thought he would take a short cut instead of keeping to the high road.

Well, that's just where Benjamin Ram went wrong, because in an hour or two he had lost his way! He went this way, and he went that way, and he went the other way, but all the same he

was lost. Some folks might have sat right down and shouted and yelled to see if they couldn't wake up their friends, but old man Ram didn't. He hadn't got a wrinkle on his horn for nothing.

He just stuck his chin in the wind, he did, and he marched right on. He kept on and on, and it wasn't long before he began to feel mighty lonesome.

He kept walking on till the night came, and still he went on, till by and by he came to a little hill. He stopped to look round, and not far off he saw a light shining. When he saw this, old Benjamin Ram clattered his hoofs together for joy, and set off to the house where the light was.

When he got there, he knocked.

"Who's that?" said a voice.

"I'm Mr. Benjamin Ram, and I've lost my way, and I've come to ask you if you can take me in for the night," said old man Ram.

"Walk right in!" called the voice. So with that he opened the door and walked in, and made a bow. But he had no sooner made his bow and looked round than he began to shiver and shake, because sitting right there in front of the fire was old Brer Bear, grinning and showing all his white teeth. And if Mr. Benjamin

Ram hadn't been so old and stiff he would have shot out of the door and away, but before he had time even to think about such a thing old Brer Bear jumped up, shut the door and fastened it with a great big chain.

Old Mr. Ram knew he was caught then, but he put a bold face on and made another low bow.

"I hope Brer Bear and Mrs. Bear and the family are well," he said. "I've just dropped in to warm myself and to ask the way to Miss Meadows'. Perhaps Brer Bear would be good enough to set me on my way again?"

"To be sure," said Brer Bear, with a grin. "Just put your walking-stick over in the corner, and set your bag on the floor, and make yourself at home. We haven't got much in the house, but what we have you shall share—for we'll take good care of you, Mr. Benjamin Ram!"

Brer Bear threw another log on the fire and slipped out to the kitchen, where he whispered to Mrs. Bear. "Old woman, old woman! Here's fresh meat come to supper!"

Poor Mr. Benjamin Ram heard the whisper and he shook in his shoes. He knew he couldn't get away, and whilst he was sitting there it crossed his mind that he might as well play one last tune on his fiddle.

With that he untied his bag and took out the fiddle. He began to tune it—*plink, plank, plunk, plink! Plunk, plank, plink, plunk!*

Now, when old Mrs. Bear heard the strange and curious noise of the fiddle being tuned up she couldn't think what in the world it was! Of course, Mr Benjamin Ram didn't know how astonished Mrs. Bear was, and he kept on tuning up, pulling the fiddle strings tighter and sounding them with his hoof—*plank, plink, plunk, plank!* Then old Mrs. Bear, she took hold of Brer Bear's arm and said:

"Hey, old man! What's that noise?"

Then both of them pricked up their ears and listened, and just then Mr. Benjamin Ram put the end of the fiddle under his chin, and began to play an old, gay tune. Well, Brer Bear and Mrs. Bear, they listened and listened, out there in the kitchen, and the harder they listened the more scared they got, because old Benjamin Ram, he just played like a madman, sort of wild and fierce, and the notes squealed and shrieked on his fiddle like hens squawking in the rain.

Then Brer Bear and Mrs. Bear couldn't stand it any longer and they took to their heels and fled to the swamp at the back of the house as if a hive of bees was after them!

Well, old man Ram went on and on fiddling, and at last he stopped. He didn't see Brer Bear anywhere, and he didn't hear Mrs. Bear. He looked in the kitchen. No bear there. He looked in the cupboard. No bear there. He looked in the back porch. No bear there either.

"Hoo!" said Mr. Benjamin Ram in surprise. "No bear here and I guess there won't be to-night if I can help it!" And with that he shut all the doors and locked them, and he hunted round and found some peas and bread in the loft. He ate them for his supper, and then he lay down by the fire and slept like a log all night through.

Next morning he awoke very early, and he set out from Brer Bear's house, and found the way to Miss Meadows'. Folks were still dancing there, and when they saw him coming in at the door they all ran to him. One took his hat, and one took his stick, and the other took his fiddle.

"Gracious goodness, Mr. Ram!" they cried. "Where in the world have you been? We're so glad you've come. Stir round, folks, and get Mr. Ram a cup of hot coffee!"

"Well, folks," said Mr. Benjamin Ram, as he put his fiddle under his chin once more, "this is the second time I've played my fiddle in a few hours—and the first time the folks shook their toes all right! They shook them so well that I never saw them again! Now then—shake your feet and let's see you dance—*plink, plonk, plank, plunk!*"

93

Brer Rabbit's Astonishing Prank

BRER RABBIT was always one for thinking out new tricks. He didn't copy anyone else, and nobody knew what he was going to do next. He was the funniest creature of the whole lot. Some folks called him lucky, and when he got in a fix he nearly always came out on top.

One time Brer Rabbit thought he'd pay a call on old Brer Bear—but he was mighty careful to make sure that Brer Bear and his family were out, before he went! He sat down by the side of the road and he watched them go by—old Brer Bear, old Mrs. Bear and the twin children, Kubs and Klibs.

Old Brer Bear and old Mrs. Bear they went on ahead and Kubs and Klibs came shuffling and scrambling along behind. When Brer Rabbit saw this, he thought that now was the time to go and pay a visit at Brer Bear's house. So off he went.

It wasn't long before he was in Brer Bear's house, sniffing here and prying there. He looked in the cupboards and he pried in the drawers. Whilst he was going around peeping here, there and everywhere, he began to feel about on the shelves, and a bucket of honey that Brer Bear had put up there fell down and spilt all over Brer Rabbit. A little more and he would have been drowned in honey! From head to heels Brer Rabbit was covered in honey; he wasn't just splashed with it, he was covered with it. He had to sit still whilst the honey dripped out of his eyes before he could see anything.

Well, after a little, he looked round and said to himself: "Heyo, there! What am I going to do now? If I go out into the sunshine the bumble bees and the flies will swarm up and take me—and if I stay here, Brer Bear will come back and catch me. I don't know what I'm a-going to do!"

By and by an idea came to Brer Rabbit, and he slipped out of Brer Bear's house and into the woods. And when he got there, what did he do but roll himself over and over in the leaves and the dust to try and rub the honey off himself. He rolled around, and the leaves all stuck to him! The more he rolled the more the leaves stuck to him, till after a while Brer Rabbit was the most curious-looking creature you ever saw! And if Miss Meadows and the girls had seen him then and there, they certainly wouldn't have asked him to call at their house any more. Indeed and they wouldn't!

Well, Brer Rabbit jumped around, he did, and tried to shake the leaves off himself. But the leaves, they weren't going to be shaken off. Brer Rabbit shook and shivered, but the leaves all stuck to him. The capers he cut out there in the woods all by himself were most astonishing! But not a leaf could he shake off.

Brer Rabbit saw that this wasn't going to be any good, so he thought he'd better be going home, and off he went. But you never saw such a strange sight in your life as Brer Rabbit looked,

stuck all over with leaves, from whiskers and ears to toes! He walked along, he did, and at every step he took, the leaves went s w i s h y - s w u s h y, splishy-splushy, and from the fuss he made and the way he looked you would have thought him the savagest creature that had lived on the earth since old man Noah turned the animals out of the Ark! And if you had met him you wouldn't have been with him long! You'd have run away as fast as could be.

Well, the first person Brer Rabbit met was old Sis Cow, and no sooner did she lay eyes on him than she threw up her tail and raced away as if a pack of dogs was after her! This made Brer Rabbit laugh, because he knew that if a sensible old creature like Sis Cow ran away like mad in the broad daylight, there must be something mighty curious-looking about the leaves stuck all over him.

The next person Brer Rabbit met was a girl carrying a basket of corn and a basket of piglets, and when she saw Brer Rabbit coming prancing and dancing along, she flung down her baskets and fairly flew down the road! And the piglets, they set off through the wood, and such a noise as they made with their running and their snorting and their squealing has never been heard before or since!

It went on like this whenever Brer Rabbit met anybody— they just turned and ran for their lives!

Of course, this made Brer Rabbit feel mighty biggitty, and

he thought it would be a good joke to drop round and see old Brer Fox. And whilst he stood there thinking about this, along came Brer Bear and all his family. Brer Rabbit grinned to himself, and started off across the road towards Brer Bear.

Old Brer Bear stopped and looked at him, and Brer Rabbit went nearer and nearer. Old Mrs. Bear stood it as long as she could and then she threw down her sunshade and climbed up a tree! Brer Bear looked as if he was not going to run away, but when Brer Rabbit jumped straight up into the air and gave himself a shake that set the leaves going swishy-swushy, splishy-splushy, well, old Brer Bear gave a grunt and tore down a whole fence, trying to get away from Brer Rabbit. And Kubs and Klibs, they took their hats in their hands and they went skaddling through the bushes like a pack of horses!

Well, Brer Rabbit paraded on down the road, and by and by he came across Brer Fox and Brer Wolf, who were busy fixing up a plan to catch Brer Rabbit, and they didn't see Brer Rabbit till they were right up to him! And goodness! When they saw him they gave him all the room he wanted!

Brer Wolf, he tried to show off, he did, because he wanted to look biggitty in front of Brer Fox, and he stopped and asked Brer Rabbit who he was. Well, old Brer Rabbit, he jumped up and down in the middle of the road, till all the leaves on him went swishy-swushy, splishy-splushy, and he shouted out:

"Oh, I'm the Wull-of-the-Wust! I'm the Wull-of-the-Wust, and you're the man I'm after!"

Then Brer Rabbit made as if he were going to jump at Brer Fox and Brer Wolf, and the way those two creatures ran for their lives was a sight to see!

Brer Rabbit got home at last and gave himself a good wash. And a long time after that, it happened that Brer Rabbit came up behind Brer Fox and Brer Wolf, and he hid behind a tree-stump and yelled out:

"I'm the Wull-of-the-Wust, and you're the men I'm after!"

Brer Fox and Brer Wolf shot off in a great fright, but before they had gone very far Brer Rabbit ran from behind the stump and waved to them—and he laughed fit to kill himself when he saw the surprised faces of Brer Fox and Brer Wolf.

Brer Rabbit told Miss Meadows about it, and the next time Brer Fox called, the girls began to giggle and laugh. And then they asked Brer Fox to be careful, in case the Wull-of-the-Wust dropped in. But Brer Fox looked mighty glum, he did, and just vowed to himself he would get even with Brer Rabbit, if it took him a month of Sundays to do it!

Brer Fox Tricks Brer Terrapin

BRER FOX HAD been tricked so many times by Brer Rabbit that he just longed to trick somebody himself, to show he could be clever when he wanted to.

So he looked round to see which of the other creatures he could trick, and one day, when he was going along the road, he met old Brer Terrapin. Well, Brer Fox thought it would be very easy to trick Brer Terrapin because he was so slow and Brer Fox thought it would be fine to play a joke on him.

So he marched up to Brer Terrapin, mighty biggitty, and called to him:

"How do you find yourself this morning, Brer Terrapin?"

"Slow, Brer Fox, mighty slow," said Brer Terrapin. "Day in and day out I'm mighty slow, and it looks as if I'm getting slower. I'm slow and poorly, Brer Fox. How do you feel yourself?"

"Oh, I'm up-and-doing, same as I always am," said Brer Fox. "What makes your eyes so red, Brer Terrapin?"

"It's all the trouble I see," said Brer Terrapin. "I see trouble, Brer Fox, and you see none. Trouble comes to me, and piles up on trouble!"

"Good gracious, Brer Terrapin, you don't know what trouble is," said Brer Fox. "If you want to see some sure-enough trouble, you should come along with me. I'm the man that can show you trouble!

"Well, then," said Brer Terrapin, "if you're the man that can show me trouble, then I'm the man that wants to have a look at it!

"Well, have you seen the Old Scarecrow?" asked Brer Fox.

"No, but I've heard tell of him," said Brer Terrapin.

"Well, the Old Scarecrow is the kind of trouble I'm telling you about," said Brer Fox. "If you want to see trouble, you just come along with me and I'll take you up to the broom-sage field, and we'll wait there a while and it won't be any time before we catch sight of the Old Scarecrow. Then you'll know what trouble is all right, Brer Terrapin."

Now Brer Terrapin couldn't help feeling there was something wrong somewhere, but he was too flat-footed to have any scuffle with Brer Fox, and he said to himself he'd better go along with him and just trust to luck. So they went along and came to the fence round the broom-sage field.

"You help me over the fence and maybe I'll see the Old Scarecrow somewhere about," said Brer Terrapin.

Well, as soon as Brer Terrapin was in the field across the fence, looking out for the scarecrow that wasn't there, Brer Fox set out to make some trouble for poor Brer Terrapin. He rushed off to Miss Meadows' house and asked her for a piece of burning wood to light his pipe.

He took the chunk of wood, ran back to the field and set the dry grass there on fire—and it wasn't long before it looked as if the whole field would blaze up!

Now, when old Brer Terrapin had gone across the fence and had begun to wade through the grass the very first person he met there was Brer Rabbit, lying asleep on the shady side of a tussock of grass. Brer Rabbit always slept with one eye open, and he was awake as soon as he heard Brer Terrapin scuffling and scrambling along. They shook hands with one another and said "Howdy?"

As they were talking they saw the field getting afire, and Brer Terrapin was scared stiff.

"Don't you worry now, Brer Terrapin," said Brer Rabbit. "This is the trouble that Brer Fox sent you to look for! Well, it's a blessing you met me, Brer Terrapin, because if you hadn't you'd have been roasted to death!"

This made Brer Terrapin more scared than ever, and he said he wanted to get out of the field. But Brer Rabbit said he'd take care of him, and he took Brer Terrapin to the middle of the field, where there was a big hollow tree-stump. Brer Rabbit lifted

Brer Terrapin on to this stump, and Brer Terrapin slipped down into the hole. Brer Rabbit crept in after him, and when the fire came a-snipping and a-snapping round they sat as safe in the stump as a bird in its nest!

When the fire was over Brer Terrapin looked round, and he saw Brer Fox running up and down outside the fence as if he were looking for something inside the field.

Then Brer Rabbit, he stuck his head up out of the hole and saw Brer Fox too, and he began to shout in a squeaky voice like Brer Terrapin's: "Brer Fox! Oh, Brer Fox! Come over here to this tree-stump. I've got Brer Rabbit caught in here!"

And when Brer Fox heard that he jumped over the fence and landed down on the half-burnt grass. It hurt him so much and stung his feet so hard that he squealed and rolled over. And the more he rolled, the more he burnt himself, and Brer Rabbit and Brer Terrapin they shouted and laughed till they couldn't laugh any more.

When Brer Fox got out of the field at last and went limping down the road, old Brer Terrapin yelled after him:

"Oh, there's trouble here, for sure, Brer Fox, and you found it, didn't you? Oh, you found it all right, Brer Fox, so you did!"

Brer Rabbit's Shilling

NOW ONCE IT HAPPENED that the snow fell very thickly, and Brer Rabbit's house was white from roof to door. Brer Rabbit looked out of the window and sighed.

"I'll have to get out my broom and do a bit of sweeping," he said. "My arms aren't so strong as they used to be. I don't reckon I want to sweep too long—but who is there who would do it for me?"

He sat and thought for a while, and then he pulled his whiskers and smiled.

"Maybe I'll get someone to do my sweeping after all!" he said. "We'll see!"

He put on his hat and coat and scarf and sat by his window, watching for the creatures to go by on their way to market. As soon as he saw somebody ambling along in the distance, he skipped out into his front garden. But he didn't take his broom. No—he put his hands in his pockets, hunched up his shoulders, and went up and down his garden path, shuffling with his feet in the snow, as if he were looking for something.

Presently along came Brer Fox. He looked over the wall and greeted Brer Rabbit.

"Heyo, Brer Rabbit! You look as if you've lost something!"

"Do I?" said Brer Rabbit. "Well, maybe you're right and maybe you're wrong."

"Shall I come in and help you look for it?" said Brer Fox, obligingly. He felt certain that Brer Rabbit wouldn't be out in his garden on such a cold morning, if what he had lost wasn't worth hunting for. "Maybe you've lost a shilling?"

"Maybe I have and maybe I haven't!" said Brer Rabbit. "That's neither here nor there. I'm thinking of getting a broom and

sweeping this snow away. Then if I've lost anything, maybe I'll find it. But my arms are tired this morning, so I thought I'd just have a look first, before sweeping."

"Oh, are your arms tired?" said Brer Fox. "Well, see here, Brer Rabbit, I'll do a bit of sweeping for you. My arms are as strong as anything. You get me a broom and I'll be pleased to do a bit of sweeping."

Brer Rabbit grinned to himself. He knew that Brer Fox only meant to do the sweeping because he hoped to find what was lost! He went to his shed and fetched out a mighty big broom.

"Here you are," he said to Brer Fox. "I'd think it mighty kind of you if you'd do a bit of sweeping, mighty kind!"

"Don't mention it," said Brer Fox, politely. He took the broom and began to sweep, keeping a sharp eye open for any money that might be buried beneath the snow.

Pretty soon along came Brer Bear, and he looked in astonishment at the sight of Brer Fox sweeping up Brer Rabbit's snow, for it was well known that the two were enemies.

"What are you doing that for?" he asked Brer Bear.

"Oh, Brer Rabbit's lost a shilling in the snow," grinned Brer Fox. "And maybe I'll find it. If I do, Brer Rabbit won't see it again!"

"Hooo! A silver shilling!" said Brer Bear, surprised. "Well—in that case I think I'll run along and get my broom too. I could do with a silver shilling, so I could."

And to Brer Fox's disgust Brer Bear went along home, found a broom, and came back with it. Soon he was sweeping hard, listening for the tinkle of a shilling. Brer Rabbit looked out of his window and grinned away to himself when he saw the two of them so hard at work. They had already swept halfway down his path to the gate.

Not long after this, Brer Possum came along, and how he stared to see Brer Fox and Brer Bear sweeping so busily in Brer Rabbit's garden!

"What's all this?" he asked. "Is Brer Rabbit ill or something? What are you sweeping his path for? Not out of the kindness of your hearts, I guess!"

"You be quiet," said Brer Fox, with a grin. "We're hunting for a shilling that Brer Rabbit dropped in the snow. He thinks we're sweeping to save his poor tired arms—but we're not!

"Well, I guess I'll join in," said Brer Possum, at once. A shilling meant a lot of money to old Brer Possum. My, what couldn't he buy at the market for a shilling!

He saw Brer Rabbit at the window and he shouted to him: "Heyo, Brer Rabbit! Sorry to hear your arms are bad. I don't mind giving a hand with your snow if you've got a broom to lend me!"

Brer Rabbit opened the window and threw out another broom. "Thanks, Brer Possum," he said. "I didn't know I'd got such good friends."

So in half a minute Brer Possum was also sweeping hard—swish, swish, swish, went the three brooms, and Brer Rabbit sat at his window and hugged himself, watching the workers panting and puffing in his garden. Now, when his path was swept quite clean, right to his gate, Brer Rabbit threw open his window.

"You *are* good friends!" he said. "Don't you stop to do any more. I'm much obliged to you. Shut the gate after you, please!"

"Well! Hark at that!" said Brer Fox, indignantly. "Doesn't offer us a cup of tea even! To think of all the hard work we've done for nothing—and we haven't even found the shilling!"

Brer Fox went to the window, and Brer Rabbit hurriedly shut it down. Brer Fox looked in. He saw Brer Rabbit put his hands into his pockets—he saw him give a delighted grin. He saw him pull out a bright shining shilling and hold it up to look at it.

"It was in my pocket after all!" shouted Brer Rabbit through the window. "Think of that now! It was in my pocket all the time! Well, well, well!"

Brer Fox glared at him. "I don't believe you ever did drop it in the snow," he said.

"Well, of course I didn't," said Brer Rabbit, in a surprised voice. "Whatever made you think that? Dear, dear—you surely haven't been sweeping my snow just to find a shilling you thought I'd dropped, have you? And I thought you were all doing it out of kindness, so I did!"

Brer Fox was so angry that he threw Brer Rabbit's broom up on to his roof. He stalked out of the gate, and Brer Bear and Brer Possum went with him.

"If I wasn't tired out, I'd sweep all the snow back again on to his path!" grumbled Brer Bear. "That creature's sharper than a knife!"

Brer Rabbit laughed loudly when he saw the three marching out of his front gate, down a nicely-swept path. "Thanks!" he called out. "Come again to-morrow if the snow falls to-night!"

He had to get a ladder and fetch his best broom down from the roof. But he didn't mind that, not he! He'd got his path swept for nothing, clever old Brer Rabbit!

Brer Bear Goes to the Well

ONE DAY IT HAPPENED that Brer Rabbit met old Brer Bear ambling along, and he skipped up to him.

"Good-day, Brer Bear," said Brer Rabbit. "How's yourself?"

"Oh, up and down, up and down," said Brer Bear. "So you're not caught yet, Brer Rabbit? My, it just beats me how you manage to skip about as you do, the biggest scamp in the woods, and never get caught."

Well, Brer Bear, *you'll* never catch me!" said Brer Rabbit. "I'm too smart for you. You're slow in your feet and slow in your mind too. I'm quick in my feet and quick in my mind! No one's any match for me, not even Brer Fox!"

Now it doesn't do to boast, not even if you are as clever as Brer Rabbit. Something horrid always happens to boasters—and no sooner were the words out of Brer Rabbit's mouth, than Brer Fox popped out from behind a tree and caught him by the back of the neck!

"*I'm* pretty quick on my feet this morning, Brer Rabbit," grinned Brer Fox. "Oh yes—I heard you coming along boasting so loudly that you didn't see me hiding behind that tree. You didn't see Brer Bear wink at me. So we are too slow for you, are we? Well, this time you're wrong. You're going home with me—and you're going to be cooked for my dinner!"

"Let me have a share," begged Brer Bear. "You can't eat all of him. He's pretty fat."

"Well, you come along too, then," said Brer Fox, swinging Brer Rabbit to and fro in a way that made him very angry indeed. They went along to Brer Fox's house, and Brer Fox shut all the windows tight and locked the door. Then he dumped Brer Rabbit into a cupboard and shut the door.

Now no sooner did Brer Rabbit get into that cupboard than he began to scurry round and round it, making all kinds of excited squeals and squeaks. Brer Fox and Brer Bear were astonished.

"Now what's the matter, Brer Rabbit?" said Brer Fox at last.

"There's an enormous fat mouse in here," panted Brer Rabbit. "My, he *is* fat. I thought maybe I could catch him and eat him."

"Don't you do anything of the sort," said Brer Fox fiercely. "Any mouse in my cupboard is *mine*. I'll open the door and you shoo him out."

So Brer Fox opened the door, but no mouse came out. "He's gone into that box," said Brer Rabbit.

Brer Fox took up the box—and at the same moment Brer Rabbit shot out of that cupboard into the kitchen. He looked around for a hiding-place, and saw Brer Fox's big old boiling-saucepan set ready at the side of the fireplace. He slipped the lid to one side and jumped in. Then he slipped the lid on and lay in that saucepan as quiet as could be.

Well, Brer Fox and Brer Bear were so busy looking for that mouse that at first they didn't bother about where Brer Rabbit had gone. "He can't get away," said Brer Fox. "The windows are fastened, and the door is locked."

Well, they didn't find that mouse, of course, because there never had been one there. It was just a trick of old Brer Rabbit's to get out of the cupboard.

"A silly trick!" said Brer Fox. "He may get out of the cupboard—but he can't get out of my kitchen! My word, when I find him I'll give him such a spanking that he won't know whether he is standing on his head or his heels!"

Brer Fox began to look for Brer Rabbit. He couldn't find him. "Well, he's here somewhere," he said to Brer Bear, "and when I find him I'll pop him into my saucepan and boil him for our dinner. I hope he's trembling when he hears that!"

Brer Rabbit lay low in the saucepan and didn't say a word.

Brer Fox was angry. He turned to Brer Bear who was standing doing nothing to help.

"Don't stand there doing nothing!" he said. "Go to the well and fill the saucepan with water. Then it will be ready to boil Brer Rabbit in when I find him. And go out of the door quickly in case Brer Rabbit makes a run for it."

Brer Bear picked up the saucepan—with Brer Rabbit in it, of course—and went to the door. He opened it quickly, got through it as fast as he could, and shut it behind him.

"I'll have found Brer Rabbit by the time you get back!" Brer Fox shouted after him, and began to hunt everywhere again. But it wasn't much good looking in the kitchen for Brer Rabbit—he was going to the well in the saucepan. He felt very pleased with himself.

He began to jiggle the lid up and down. "Jiggle-jiggle-jing!" went the lid. "Jiggle-jiggle-jing!"

Brer Bear looked down, surprised. He wasn't used to saucepans behaving like that. He took hold of the lid and set it on very firmly indeed. But old Brer Rabbit pushed it loose again, and "Jiggle-jiggle-jing!" it went, "jiggle-jiggle-jing!"

Brer Bear set the saucepan down on the ground and put the lid on as hard as he could. And as he pushed it on, Brer Rabbit pushed it off. So it felt to Brer Bear as if the lid was being very obstinate, and he began to shout angrily at the saucepan.

"How dare you behave like that? You keep your lid on properly!"

"Shan't!" shouted Brer Rabbit in a voice as like a saucepan as he could manage.

Brer Bear nearly fell over with surprise when the saucepan answered him back. He sat down and stared at it.

"Don't you dare to be cheeky to a smart fellow like *me!*" he said to the saucepan.

"Smart fellow, did you say?" said Brer Rabbit, still pretending to be the saucepan. "Well, do you think it's smart to let old Brer Fox order you off to the well, so that he can find Brer Rabbit and gobble him up before you come back? That's what he's doing, for sure!"

"Well, stars and moon, I never thought of that!" said stupid old Brer Bear, getting up. "I'll just go right back and see if I catch him eating up Brer Rabbit!"

He ambled back to Brer Fox's house and opened the door. Brer Fox was looking puzzled. He had hunted everywhere for Brer Rabbit, and hadn't found him. He stared at Brer Bear.

"You're back quickly," he said. "Where's the saucepan?"

"That *saucepan* told me something queer," said Brer Bear. "It told me you had ordered me off to the well for water so that you could gobble up Brer Rabbit by yourself."

"The saucepan told you!" said Brer Fox, in astonishment. "Are you mad, Brer Bear? Saucepans don't talk."

"Yours does," said Brer Bear. "I heard it. It's a mighty cheeky saucepan, too. If it were mine I wouldn't have it in my house."

"Brer Bear, I tell you saucepans don't talk," said Brer Fox. Then a thought flashed into his mind, and he stared at Brer Bear in dismay. "Brer Bear! That wasn't the saucepan. It was Brer Rabbit! He hid in the saucepan! You took him out in it! And he cheeked you, and sent you back here so that he could escape. Quick—where did you leave the saucepan? Maybe he couldn't get the lid off and is still there!"

So the two of them rushed out to the saucepan—but as you can guess, it was quite empty! Brer Rabbit was gone.

"You're just as stupid as ever!" shouted Brer Fox to Brer Bear.

"Well, you're not very smart yourself, to tell me to go out to the well with the saucepan—and Brer Rabbit inside it all the time!" said Brer Bear.

A voice floated down to them from far up the hill. This is what it sang:

> *"Slow in your feet*
> *And slow in your mind,*
> *Always too late, always behind!*
> *But I'm quick in my mind,*
> *And quick in my feet,*
> *Oh, Brer Rabbit finds you all easy to beat!"*

"Well, you can guess who *that* is, Brer Bear," said Brer Fox, with a nasty look. And Brer Bear *could* guess—quite easily!

Brer Rabbit Goes to the Party

IT HAPPENED ONE TIME that Brer Fox gave a party, and asked Brer Bear, Brer Wolf, Brer Raccoon and some others. But he didn't ask Brer Rabbit. All the same, when Brer Rabbit heard about it, he made up his mind to go! Well, those that had been invited went to Brer Fox's, and Brer Fox asked them in and got them chairs, and they sat there, laughing and talking. Then by and by Brer Fox put out some food and drink, and told them to help themselves.

Well, whilst they were eating and drinking, what do you suppose Brer Rabbit was doing? Oh, he was sailing round as usual, fixing up his tricks! He had been looking for a big drum he had, and when he found it he fixed it on to the front of him and made his way down the road to Brer Fox's.

As he went he beat the drum till it sounded like a mixture of hail and thunder. My, what a noise it made! It went like this:

"Diddybum, diddybum, diddybum-bum-bum—diddybum!"

Well, all the creatures were eating and drinking and laughing, and they didn't hear any noise, but all the same here came Brer Rabbit:

"Diddybum, diddybum, diddybum-bum-bum—diddybum!"

By and by, Brer Raccoon, who always had sharp ears, asked Brer Fox what that noise was, and by that time all the animals stopped to listen. And along came Brer Rabbit, beating that drum like thunder and hail!

"Diddybum, diddybum, diddybum-bum-bum—diddybum!"

The creatures kept on listening to this loud and curious noise, and Brer Rabbit got nearer and nearer. Soon Brer Raccoon reached under his chair for his hat.

"Well, Brer Fox," said he, all of a shiver and shake, "I expect

I'd better be going. I told my old woman I wouldn't be a minute, and here I've been two or three hours!"

With that Brer Raccoon skipped out—but he hadn't got much farther than the back gate before all the others joined him, running along as if they were in a race, and old Brer Fox leading them, looking as scared as could be! My, he didn't know what that noise was, and he didn't mean to wait and see, either!

Off the animals went, tumbling over one another, and scrambling about in alarm till they got to the woods.

Old Brer Rabbit came on down the road—diddybum, diddybum, diddybum-bum-bum—diddybum—and goodness gracious, when he came to Brer Fox's house there was nobody there! Brer Rabbit rapped on the open door and shouted: "Is there anyone at home?" And then he answered himself. "No, Brer Rabbit, the folks are all out!"

Then Brer Rabbit began to laugh, he did, fit to kill himself, and then he kicked Brer Fox's door wide open and marched in. He yelled, "Heyo, Brer Fox!" But there was nobody there, as he very well knew. So Brer Rabbit walked in and took a chair and made himself at home, even putting his feet up on the sofa!

He hadn't sat there long before he saw the good things on the table! So up he got and he was soon tucking into the food and drink as if he hadn't had a meal for a twelvemonth!

All this time the other creatures were hiding in the bushes listening for the diddybum, and getting ready to rush off at the least sound. But they didn't hear anything more, so Brer Fox said he was going back to the house, and who was going with him?

They all started out, they did, and they crept towards Brer Fox's house, but they were mighty slow and careful, and if a leaf had fallen off a bush, well, you wouldn't have seen any of the creatures for dust! They heard no noise, and they kept on creeping till they got to the house.

When they got there the first thing they saw was old Brer Rabbit standing by the table, stuffing himself full of good things. Brer Fox just stood by the door, staring at Brer Rabbit, and he snapped his jaws together and shouted loudly.

"Ah yi, Brer Rabbit! Many a time you escaped, but this time I've got you!"

Well, everyone shot in and got hold of old Brer Rabbit, and there he was properly caught. Brer Bear put on his spectacles and looked round at the company and said that any man caught stealing his neighbour's goods must be drowned.

"That's right enough," said Brer Fox at once. "Sure, that's right enough, Brer Bear. Brer Rabbit will have to be drowned."

Then Brer Rabbit pretended to be scared, and he squealed and cried and shouted and begged them, in the name of goodness, not to fling him into the pond because they all knew he couldn't swim.

"But if you've made up your minds to throw me in, then for pity's sake give me a walking-stick to hold on to whilst I'm a-drowning," said Brer Rabbit.

Old Brer Bear looked sternly at Brer Rabbit. "Seeing it's the last thing you'll have, you can have a stick," he said. So Brer Fox gave him one. And then they put Brer Rabbit into a wheelbarrow and wheeled him along to the pond and threw him into the water.

Well, Brer Rabbit landed on his feet, as light as a cat, and picked his way out of the pond with the help of the walking-stick! The water was so shallow that it hardly came over Brer Rabbit's shoes, and when he got out on the other side, he waved his stick to Brer Fox and grinned.

"So long, Brer Fox!" he called. "So long! Thanks for the nice party!"

Brer Fox and Brer Terrapin

ONCE BRER TERRAPIN found some big quill-feathers that had belonged to Brer Turkey Buzzard. They were lying on the ground, and Brer Terrapin picked them up. When he found that they were hollow, he blew down them.

A merry whistling noise came from them, and Brer Terrapin was delighted. He went down the road, whistling and singing loudly. And this was the song he sang:

> *Brer Terrapin's clever, Brer Terrapin's strong,*
> *He can run a swift race, he can sing a loud song,*
> *Tirallee, tirallee, tirallee, too,*
> *Brer Terrapin's smarter than you, than you!*

Well, Brer Terrapin sang this song to Brer Fox when he met him, and Brer Fox didn't like it. He sang and whistled it to Brer Bear, and Brer Bear shouted at him. He whistled and sang it to Brer Rabbit, but Brer Rabbit just didn't take any notice at all.

Soon all the animals got angry when they heard Brer Terrapin coming along with his quill-pipes, whistling how clever and smart he was. They looked for some quill-feathers for themselves, but they couldn't find any.

Brer Fox asked Brer Turkey Buzzard if he would lend him some quills, but Brer Buzzard said no, he needed all he had got. Brer Fox said couldn't he spare a few, and Brer Buzzard said, well, Brer Fox could come and have a look to see if any of his quills were good enough. But when Brer Fox got near and was looking at his feathers, Brer Turkey Buzzard flapped his wings hard in Brer Fox's face and nearly blew his whiskers off! Then away he sailed into the air, squawking with laughter.

Well, Brer Fox saw that he wouldn't be able to get any quills out of Brer Buzzard. He wanted them so badly that he went to find Brer Terrapin.

"Will you sell those quill-pipes?" said Brer Fox.

But Brer Terrapin, he held on to those quills tightly, and said no, they weren't for sale.

"Well, will you lend them for a week, then?" asked Brer Fox. "I'd like to play tunes on them to my children."

Brer Terrapin shook his head. He knew very well he wouldn't get them back once he had lent them to old Brer Fox. And as soon as Brer Fox had turned away to go, Brer Terrapin began to whistle his song.

"Brer Terrapin's clever, Brer Terrapin's strong!" But when he saw Brer Fox turning back, he took the quills out of his mouth and hid them away carefully in his shell. He knew old Brer Fox well enough!

Now Brer Fox worried and worried about those quills, and made up his mind to get them somehow. So one day he set out to find Brer Terrapin again, and when he had come across him, he began to talk to him very politely.

"How are you feeling today, Brer Terrapin?" he asked.

"Not too bad, and not too good, Brer Fox," said Brer Terrapin, putting his head inside his shell for safety.

"And how are all your family, Brer Terrapin?" said Brer Fox, coming a bit nearer.

"So-so, so-so," said Brer Terrapin, putting his little tail inside his shell.

"Brer Terrapin, could you let me have a look at those buzzard quills of yours?" said Brer Fox, not coming any nearer at all. "You see, I have goose feathers at home, and if I could see your quills closely, maybe I could make my goose feathers into quill-pipes like yours. You know how badly I've wanted your quills, Brer Terrapin. Well, just show me them and maybe I can make some like them."

Well, Brer Terrapin thought about this, with his head and his tail tucked safely away in his shell. He was a kind fellow, and he liked to do what people asked, if he could. And he didn't see why Brer Fox shouldn't see his quill-pipes, if he wanted to make some like them. So by and by he held out the quills for Brer Fox to see.

Brer Fox bent down close—and then, quick as

lightning, he jerked the quills out of Brer Terrapin's hand, picked them up, and dashed off as quick as could be! Brer Terrapin shouted after him as loud as he could yell, but he knew it was no good. He didn't even bother to go after Brer Fox, because he knew he couldn't catch him. So he just sat there, looking as if he'd lost all the friends he had in the world. Poor Brer Terrapin!

Well, Brer Fox was pleased to have got the quill-pipes, and he marched around, feeling mighty biggitty, singing and whistling. And every time he met old Brer Terrapin he played on the pipes and sang this song:

> *Brer Fox is clever, Brer Fox is strong,*
> *He can run a swift race, he can sing a loud song.*
> *Poor old Brer Terrapin, what will he do?*
> *Brer Fox is smarter than you, than you!*

And Brer Fox, he danced round and round old Brer Terrapin till Brer Terrapin had to shut his eyes, he felt so giddy! But he didn't say a word, though he felt so bad.

At last, one day when old Brer Terrapin was sitting on a log sunning himself, Brer Fox came up again, playing the same old song. But Brer Terrapin he stayed still. Brer Fox came a little nearer and played more loudly, but Brer Terrapin, he kept his eyes shut and stayed quiet.

Brer Fox came nearer still and climbed up on the log beside Brer Terrapin. Brer Terrapin said nothing. Brer Fox pushed himself nearer to him on the log and played the song again. And still Brer Terrapin said nothing.

"Heyo!" said Brer Fox, at last, rather out of breath with all his whistling. "Brer Terrapin's mighty sleepy this morning!"

Brer Terrapin kept his eyes shut and stayed as still as the log. Brer Fox got nearer and nearer to him, trying to see if he was really asleep—till suddenly Brer Terrapin opened both his eyes

and his mouth, and made a grab at Brer Fox. But he missed him! Brer Fox laughed fit to kill himself, and marched off, playing the same old tune.

Next morning Brer Terrapin sat and thought for a while—and then he went to a mud-hole and wallowed in it, rolling over and over, smearing himself with mud till he looked exactly like a clod of earth. Then he crawled out of the mud-hole and lay down under a log on which he knew Brer Fox sat every morning when he brushed out his fur.

Well, Brer Terrapin lay there, he did, and after a bit, along came Brer Fox. He sat down on the log and began to swing himself forwards and backwards. Brer Terrapin took a look at him and crept a little nearer. Brer Fox didn't see him. He thought Brer Terrapin was just a lump of dirt.

At last Brer Terrapin had crept just underneath Brer Fox's foot—and he opened his mouth and made a grab at him—and caught him by the foot!

Well, once Brer Terrapin caught hold of anything, nothing but thunder and lightning would make him leave go! He just sat there and held on to Brer Fox's foot, and Brer Fox, he jumped and jerked about, but Brer Terrapin wouldn't let him go.

"Brer Terrapin, please let me go!" yelled Brer Fox.

Then Brer Terrapin talked away down in his throat, because his mouth was over Brer Fox's foot.

"Give me my quills!"

"Leave go, and I'll go and fetch them," said Brer Fox.

"Give me my quills!"

"Do pray let me go and get them!"

"Give me my quills!"

That was all that Brer Fox could get out of Brer Terrapin! At last Brer Fox's foot hurt him so much that he had to do something about it, and he shouted out to his old woman to bring him the quills. But she was busy about the house and didn't hear him. So he called Toby, his son.

"Toby! Oh, Toby!"

"What do you want, Daddy?" shouted Toby.

"Fetch Brer Terrapin's quills."

"What's that you say, Daddy? Fetch you some pills?"

"No, you turnip-head! Fetch Brer Terrapin's quills!"

"What's that you say, Daddy? Put something on the sills?"

"No, you snail-head! Fetch Brer Terrapin's quills!"

"What's that you say, Daddy? Something to spill?"

After a bit old Mrs. Fox heard the shouting and she listened and found out that Brer Fox was yelling for the quills. So she fetched them and took them out to Brer Terrapin. And he let go his hold of Brer Fox's foot and took them. But for a long while after that old Brer Fox walked mighty queerly—hoppitty-fetchity, hoppitty-fetchity, hoppitty-fetchity! And he didn't go near Brer Terrapin for a month of Sundays!

Brer Rabbit Tricks Brer Fox

NOW ALTHOUGH BRER RABBIT was supposed to be the only creature allowed to call on Miss Meadows and the girls, Brer Fox often used to pop in and see them, too. And he was so polite and said such smart things that Miss Meadows and the girls, they let him come as often as he liked.

Well, that didn't please Brer Rabbit, who liked to be the only one around. And soon Brer Rabbit began to think how he might put a stop to Brer Fox's visits.

As he was sitting down by the side of the road, thinking this, and thinking that, fixing up his tricks, he heard a clatter up the long green lane, and along came old Brer Fox—*too-bookity-bookity-bookity-book!* He was galloping along like a pony in the field, and he was all smartened up, too, looking as slick and as shiny as if he'd just come out of a shop window!

"Where are you a-going, Brer Fox?" asked Brer Rabbit.

"I'm a-going to take dinner at Miss Meadows'," said Brer Fox, grinning at Brer Rabbit.

"That's a pity, Brer Fox," said Brer Rabbit. "I'd got some mighty good news for you!"

"What's that?" said Brer Fox.

"Well," said Brer Rabbit, scratching his ear with his hind foot, "I was taking a walk the day before yesterday when I suddenly saw the biggest and the fattest bunch of grapes that ever I laid eyes on! They were so fat and so big that the juice was just dropping out of them. The bees and the wasps were swarming there after the sweetness, and little old Jack Sparrow and his family were all there, dipping their beaks into the juice!"

Well, when Brer Fox heard this his mouth began to water, and he looked most kindly at Brer Rabbit. He sidled up to him and said:

"Come on, Brer Rabbit! Let's both go and get those grapes before they are all gone!"

Old Brer Rabbit laughed and shook his head. "I'm hungry myself," he said, "but I don't like grapes. I'm just a-rushing round to find a bit of parsley to keep the breath in my body! And if you go alone, Brer Fox, and get those grapes, what will Miss Meadows and the girls do? They are expecting you to dinner, you said."

"Oh, well, I can drop round and see them after I've had the grapes," said Brer Fox.

"Well, all right, then," said Brer Rabbit. "I'll just tell you how to find them. You know that place where you went blackberrying for Miss Meadows?"

"Yes," said Brer Fox, listening carefully.

"Well, the grapes aren't there," said Brer Rabbit. "You get to the blackberry patch, and you follow the stream there till you come to a few nut-trees—but the grapes aren't there. Then you go to the left and cross the hill till you come to a big oak-tree—but the grapes aren't there. You go down the hill till you come to another stream, and by that stream there's a dogwood tree leaning over, and by the dogwood tree is a grape-vine, and on that vine you'll find the grapes. They're so ripe that they look as

if they've all melted together, and I expect you'll find them covered with bees and wasps, but you can take that fine bushy tail of yours and brush all the insects away!"

"I'm much obliged to you," said Brer Fox, and he set off at a gallop. When he was out of sight Brer Rabbit took a blade of grass and tickled himself in the ear with it, and then he shouted and laughed and laughed and shouted till he had to lie down in the grass and get his breath back again.

After some time he jumped up and set off after Brer Fox. Brer Fox didn't look behind at all, he was so eager to find those grapes. On and on he went till he came to the dogwood tree, and near by was the grape-vine.

And sure enough, when old Brer Fox looked up at the vine, he saw what he thought was the biggest bunch of grapes he had ever seen in his life—all covered with wasps.

"Heyo!" said Brer Fox, in delight. "There's a fine bunch of grapes! And my gracious, haven't the wasps found them too! Well, I'll wipe them off with my tail."

So he balanced himself on a branch near by, and swung his big bushy tail at the bunch of grapes to brush off the wasps. But goodness gracious, no sooner had he done that than he let out a squall that Miss Meadows heard two miles away!

Old Brer Rabbit had tricked Brer Fox properly! That bunch of grapes, so fine and big, was not grapes at all, but a great big wasps' nest built in the vine! Brer Fox knocked it down with his tail, and the nest dropped right on top of him! And the wasps, they swarmed out in a rage and set to work to sting poor Brer Fox till he squealed out in fright.

Brer Fox ran, and kicked, and scratched, and bit, and scrambled, and shouted and howled, but it wasn't a bit of good. Those wasps just wouldn't leave him alone! At one time it looked as if Brer Fox was going to run towards the place where Brer Rabbit was hiding, and as soon as Brer Rabbit saw that, he was up and away! He didn't want any wasps after him! He went sailing through the woods and he didn't stop till he came to Miss Meadows' house.

"Heyo, Brer Rabbit," said Miss Meadows. "Where's Brer Fox?"

"He's gone grape-hunting," said Brer Rabbit. "I just now saw him."

"Well, to think of that!" said Miss Meadows crossly. "He said he was coming to dinner. I've done with Brer Fox. He said he'd come to dinner, and he goes off grape-hunting. Here's his dinner been ready for a long time, and we've all been waiting for Brer Fox. I shan't ask him again. You'd better stay instead, Brer Rabbit."

At first Brer Rabbit said he wouldn't stay, but by and by he took a chair and sat

127

down. He had only just begun his dinner when he saw old Brer Fox going by outside.

"There goes Brer Fox," he said to Miss Meadows and the girls. "My, isn't he fat! Looks like he's been gobbling all the grapes on the hills!"

Poor Brer Fox! He didn't want anyone to see him at all, because the wasps had stung him hard, and his head was swelled up, and his legs too.

Brer Rabbit put his head out of the door and shouted to him.

"Heyo, Brer Fox! Did you find those grapes all right?"

But Brer Fox, he didn't answer a word!

Brer Rabbit and the Moon

THERE WERE TIMES when all the creatures became friendly together and shared everything.

One time, when they were friends like this, Brer Rabbit saw that he was getting fat and lazy. This always happened when he didn't do any tricks, and the more peace there was, the worse Brer Rabbit felt. And by and by he got very restless.

When the sun shone he'd go and lie in the grass and kick at the gnats, and nibble at the mullein-stalks and wallow in the sand. But this didn't make him any thinner. One night, after supper, whilst he was running round a bit to try and get thinner, he came up with old Brer Terrapin, and after they had shaken hands and sat down on the side of the road, they began to talk about old times.

"You know, Brer Terrapin," said Brer Rabbit, at last, "I just feel I've simply got to have some fun."

"Well, Brer Rabbit," said Brer Terrapin, "then I'm the man for you to have your fun with. What are we going to do?"

"We'll play a trick on Brer Fox, Brer Wolf and Brer Bear," said Brer Rabbit. "We'll all meet down by the mill-pond tomorrow night and have a fishing-party. I'll do the talking, Brer Terrapin, and you can sit back and say 'yes' to all I say."

Brer Terrapin laughed. "If I'm not there tomorrow night you'll know a grasshopper has run off with me!" he said.

Well, Brer Rabbit set out for home, and on the way he told all the others about the fishing-party and they were pleased and promised to be at the mill-pond the next night. Miss Meadows and the girls got to hear of the party and they said they'd come along too.

Sure enough, when the time came, they were all there. Brer Bear fetched a hook and line, Brer Fox fetched a dip-net, and Brer

Terrapin fetched a box of bait.

Miss Meadows and the girls they stood by the edge of the pond and squealed every time Brer Terrapin shook the box of bait at them. Brer Bear said he was going to fish for mud-cats. Brer Wolf said he was going to get horny-heads. Brer Fox said he'd catch some perch for the ladies. Brer Terrapin said he wanted to catch minnows and Brer Rabbit winked at Brer Terrapin and said he was after a few silly-billies!

Well, they all got ready, and Brer Rabbit marched up to the pond as if he were going to throw his hook into the water—but just as he was about to fling it in he stopped and stared hard at the water as if he saw something queer there. The other creatures all stopped and watched him. Brer Rabbit dropped his rod and stood there scratching his head, looking down into the water.

Miss Meadows and the girls felt a bit uncomfortable when they saw Brer Rabbit staring hard like this. "Heyo, Brer Rabbit," they called, "what in the name of goodness is the matter with the water?"

Well, Brer Rabbit went on scratching his head and looking into the water, and by and by he took a long breath and said:

"Folks, we might just as well pack up and go home, because there won't be any fishing for us!"

With that old Brer Terrapin scrambled to the edge of the water and looked in. He shook his head, and said: "To be sure—to be sure! Tut-tut-tut! That's so, Brer Rabbit, that's surely so!" And then he crawled back again as if he were thinking hard.

"Don't be scared, folks," said Brer Rabbit. "There isn't much the matter except that the moon has dropped into the water! If you don't believe me you can look for yourself."

Well, Brer Fox looked into the pond, and said, "Well, well, well—sure enough, there's the moon!"

Brer Wolf looked in. "Mighty bad, mighty bad!" he said.

Brer Bear looked in and gave a grunt. "Who'd have thought it, who'd have thought it?" he said.

Miss Meadows and the girls looked in too and said, "Isn't it too bad!"

Then Brer Rabbit looked in again and said: "Well, folks, it's no good shaking your heads and sighing about it. Unless we get the moon out of the pond there'll be no fish for us to catch tonight! And if you ask Brer Terrapin, he'll tell you the same."

"But how can we get the moon out of the pond?" asked everyone.

"Better leave that to Brer Rabbit," said Brer Terrapin.

Brer Rabbit shut his eyes and looked as if he were thinking deeply. Then by and by he spoke. "The quickest way out of this difficulty is to send to old Mr. Mud Turtle and borrow his drag-net, and drag the moon up from there."

"Well, I'm very glad to hear you say that," said Brer Terrapin, "because old Mr. Mud Turtle is my uncle, and he'll do anything for me."

So Brer Rabbit went for the drag-net, and whilst he was gone old Brer Terrapin began to talk. "You know, folks," he said, "I've heard that those who find the moon in the water and fetch it out find a full pot of money there too! Yes, I've heard that tale time and again!"

This made Brer Fox, Brer Wolf and Brer Bear feel mighty good.

"Seeing that Brer Rabbit has been good enough to go to fetch the drag-net, we'll do the dragging," they said. When Brer Rabbit got back, he saw what was up, and he pretended he was going in after the moon, but the other creatures stopped him.

"You're a dry-foot man," they said to Brer Rabbit. "You don't like the water. We'll do the dragging for the moon."

So Brer Fox, he took hold of one end of the net, Brer Wolf took hold of the other end, and Brer Bear he waded along behind to lift the net up.

They made one haul with the net and lifted it up. No moon! They made another haul—no moon! They dragged the net again—no moon! Then by and by they waded farther out from the bank. Water ran into Brer Fox's ears, and he shook his head. Water ran into Brer Wolf's ears, and he shook his head too. Water ran into Brer Bear's ears, and he had to shake his head as well. And whilst they were all busy shaking their ears, they waded out to a very deep part where the bottom of the pond dropped right away!

Brer Fox stepped off the bottom and went right under! Brer Wolf ducked himself and went under too, and Brer Bear he plunged in and disappeared as well! And goodness gracious, they all kicked and spluttered and splashed as if they wanted to throw all the water out of the mill-pond.

When they came out Miss Meadows and the girls were laughing and giggling, and well they might, for Brer Fox, Brer Wolf and Brer Bear looked mighty queer. Brer Rabbit took a look at them, and squealed with laughter too.

"Well, folks," he said at last, "I expect we'd all better go home and get into dry clothes. Better luck next time! I hear that the

moon will take a bait of silly-billies, and it seems as if she found her bait all right tonight!"

And with that Brer Rabbit and Brer Terrapin went off to have supper with Miss Meadows and the girls, and Brer Fox, Brer Wolf and Brer Bear went off dripping—and what they said about Brer Rabbit that night would have made his ears drop off, if he could have heard!

Brer Rabbit Scares his Friends

IN THE DAYS when Brer Rabbit lived, the creatures had their ups and downs just as we do. They had their bad times and they had their good times. Some years their crops were good, and some years they were bad. Brer Rabbit was like the rest of the creatures—sometimes he had plenty of money, sometimes he had none. And when he had it he spent it.

One season Brer Rabbit did mighty well with his melons, and he said if they fetched all the money he hoped they would, he'd be able to go into town and buy a great many things.

"You do that, Mr. Rabbit, you do that," said his old woman. "You buy us all something. You get seven tin cups for the children to drink from, and seven tin plates for them to eat from, and a coffee-pot big enough for all of us."

"That's just what I'll do," said Brer Rabbit. "I'll set out for the town next Wednesday, old woman, and I'll come back with all the things you want!"

Well, Mrs. Rabbit was mighty pleased to hear this, and she slapped on her bonnet and ran up to Mrs. Mink's house to tell her all about it.

"You know, Mrs. Mink, Mr. Rabbit is going to go to town on Wednesday, and buy all the children something! What do you think of that?" said Mrs. Rabbit.

Well, Mrs. Mink was surprised to hear this, and when Brer Mink came home that night she told him about it.

"Brer Rabbit is going to town on Wednesday and is going to buy something for all his children," she said. "Why can't you buy something for *your* children, Mr. Mink, that's what I want to know!"

And then they began to quarrel, and Mr. Mink was so cross that he went out and slammed the door behind him.

Well, Mrs. Mink, she told Mrs. Fox how Brer Rabbit was going to go shopping and Mrs. Fox, she went for Brer Fox when he came home that night, and asked him why he couldn't go shopping like Brer Rabbit and bring presents home for his children!

Then Mrs. Fox told Mrs. Wolf and Mrs. Wolf told Mrs. Bear, and it wasn't long before everyone around knew that Brer Rabbit was going shopping on Wednesday and was going to bring something home for his children. And all the other creatures' children asked their daddies why they wouldn't buy them something.

Well, Brer Fox, Brer Wolf and Brer Bear felt mighty wild with Brer Rabbit for stirring up all their wives and children about his shopping.

"We'll fix up a plan to catch Brer Rabbit on his way back from town on Wednesday," said Brer Fox.

"And we'll take away everything he's bought!" grinned Brer Wolf.

"And I'd just like to see his old woman's face when she sees Brer Rabbit coming home from town without a thing after all!" said Brer Bear.

When Wednesday came, Brer Rabbit had an early breakfast

136

and set out for the town. He had plenty of money in his pocket, and he went and looked at all the shops there were. He bought himself some cigars and a red pocket handkerchief, and he bought his old woman a large coffee-pot, and he got his children seven tin cups and seven tin plates. When the sun was just going down he started out for home.

He walked along, he did, feeling mighty biggitty, but by and by he sat down under a blackjack tree, for he felt a bit tired. He fanned himself with one of the tin plates and yawned loudly.

Well, whilst he was doing this, a little tree-creeper bird ran up and down the tree behind him, making a mighty fuss. After a while Brer Rabbit got cross, and shooed him away with the tin plate. That made the little tree-creeper madder than ever, and it flew on to a branch just by Brer Rabbit's head, and sang a little song.

> *Pilly-wee, pilly-wee,*
> *I can see what you can't see!*
> *I see, pilly-wee,*
> *I see what you can't see!*

Well, he kept on like this, he did, till Brer Rabbit began to look round to see what it could be that the tree-creeper could see. And suddenly he saw marks in the sand, where someone had been sitting a little while back. And Brer Rabbit looked at these marks closely, and saw what the little tree-creeper meant!

Brer Rabbit scratched his head and spoke softly to himself.

"Ah-yi! " he said. "Here's where Brer Fox has been sitting, and there's the mark of his nice bushy tail! And here's where Brer Wolf has been sitting, and there's the mark of his fine long tail! And here's where Brer Bear's been squatting down, and there's the mark that shows he hasn't got a tail! They've all been here— and I guess they're hiding down in the hollow yonder waiting for me!"

With that Brer Rabbit put all his goods into the bushes, and crept round and about to see what he could see. And sure enough, when he crept near to the little hollow down the hill, he saw them all a-waiting for him. But they didn't see him! Brer Fox was on one side of the path, and Brer Wolf was on the other side, and Brer Bear, he was curled up, having a nap!

Well, Brer Rabbit took a peep at them, he did, and he smacked his lips and pulled his whiskers for joy. He held his hands across his mouth and laughed fit to burst himself—but he didn't make a sound!

Then off went Brer Rabbit to the bushes where he had left his goods, and when he got there he danced around, and slapped his legs and did all kinds of queer things. He meant to play a fine trick on the others!

Then he got to work. He took the coffee-pot, turned it upside down, and stuck it on his head! Then he ran a string through the handles of the tin cups and slung them across his shoulder. Then he divided the tin plates up, and took some in one hand and some in the other. When he was quite ready he crept to the top of the hill, took a running start, and flew down the hill like a hurricane—*rickety, rackety, slambang!*

Well, bless us all, the creatures had never in their lives heard a noise like that, and they hadn't seen anyone looking like Brer Rabbit, either, with the coffee-pot on his head, the cups rattling on the string, and the plates waving and shining in the air, and banging whenever Brer Rabbit clapped them together! *Rickety, rackety, slambang!*

Now old Brer Bear was taking a nap in the hollow, and the noise scared him so much that he rushed off and ran right over Brer Fox. He rushed out on to the path, but when he saw Brer Rabbit flying down towards him, looking mighty queer, he rushed off again, and fell over Brer Wolf. What with all the scrambling and scuffling, Brer Rabbit came right up to them before they could get away!

And how he shouted! Goodness gracious, you should have heard him!

"Give me room! Turn me loose! I'm old man Spewter-Splutter, with long claws and scales down my back! I'm snaggle-toothed

and double-jointed! Give me room!"

And then he'd give a yell, and bang the tin plates together and rattle all the cups—r*ickety, rackety, slambang!* And when Brer Fox, Brer Bear and Brer Wolf saw what was coming on them, they just took to their heels and ran for their lives!

Brer Bear ran straight into a tree-stump and split it into bits—and do you know, when Brer Rabbit and his children went along that way the next morning, they got enough firewood from that split stump to last them all the winter!

Ah, Brer Rabbit's a sly one, he is! There's no tricking him, that's certain!

Brer Fox is a Snowman

NOW ONCE BRER FOX thought of a very good trick to play on Brer Rabbit. He called on Brer Wolf and told him about it.

"Listen," he said. "What about you and me going along to Brer Rabbit's garden when he's out this morning and building a fine big snowman?"

"Well, there doesn't seem much sense in that," said Brer Wolf.

"Wait and let me tell you," said Brer Fox. "You see, we'll build the snowman—and then he'll see it when he comes home, and he'll laugh. And tonight I'll go along and knock it down, and stand there myself instead, with a white sheet round me. Then, when he comes out, he won't know it's me, and I can jump out on him nicely!"

"All right," said Brer Wolf. "We'll do that. We'll go right along now."

So off they both went. Brer Rabbit was out shopping, so Brer Wolf and Brer Fox had plenty of time to get to work. Snow was thick on the ground, and they soon built a fine big snowman in Brer Rabbit's garden.

"Make it as like me as you can," said Brer Fox. "Not too fat because I'm rather thin now."

Well, they finished it by the time Brer Rabbit came home, and how he laughed when he saw it. "It's a mighty good snowman, isn't it?" he said to Brer Raccoon, who was walking along with him. "I wonder who made it?"

Brer Terrapin was ambling along slowly in the snow and he called out to Brer Rabbit. "I know who made it. Brer Wolf and Brer Fox did!"

Brer Rabbit stared at the snowman and grew very thoughtful. "Now why did Brer Wolf and Brer Fox trouble themselves to

come and build a snowman in my garden?" he said. "Now, I just do wonder why?"

The more he thought about it, the more he wondered. He felt quite uncomfortable about it. "I think somehow I'll send a note along to Mr. Dog, and ask him to keep me company tonight," he thought. "Mr. Dog's so sensible and wise. I shall feel safe with him. I can't help feeling there is something tricky about that snowman, for all he's made of soft white snow."

So he sent a note along and asked Mr. Dog to come along that night and have supper with him. And Mr. Dog arrived in good time, with his tail brushed, and a very smart new collar on.

Now, as the two of them were having supper, Old Brer Fox crept up outside, and knocked down the big snowman. He had a big white sheet wrapped around himself. He had cut two holes for eyes so that he could look through them. He stood himself up in the same place where the snowman had been and he waited.

There was a light in Brer Rabbit's house, so Brer Fox knew Brer Rabbit was there. He stood out there in the cold moonlight and wondered how to get old Brer Rabbit out in the garden so that he could pounce on him.

"I'll sing a song," thought Brer Fox. "He will think it's a poor old beggar-man singing for money. He'll either come out to give him money, or he'll come out to chase him away."

So Brer Fox lifted up his voice and sang.

> *"I'm out in the moo-oo-oonlight,*
> *A beggar-man worn and old,*
> *I'm shivering down to my shoo-oe-soles*
> *Because I'm so terribly cold.*
> *Ooooooh! Ooooooh! Ooooooh!"*

Brer Rabbit and Mr. Dog were most surprised to hear this song. They pricked up their ears and listened.

"Funny," said Brer Rabbit. "Beggar-men don't usually come around singing at this time of night."

"It sounds a bit like Brer Fox's voice," said Mr. Dog, listening.

"It does," said Brer Rabbit. "He's been looking out for me lately. He doesn't like me, Mr. Dog."

"I know," said Mr. Dog, grinning. "I'm not surprised. You've played some mighty good tricks on him, Brer Rabbit."

"Will you come out and see if the old beggar-man is Mr. Fox?" asked Brer Rabbit.

Mr. Dog had had a mighty good supper, and he was feeling grateful to Brer Rabbit. He nodded his big head. "Yes, I'll come along," he said.

So the two went to the door and opened it. When Brer Fox saw that Mr. Dog was there too he was startled. He didn't like Mr. Dog at all. Mr. Dog could run fast and always chased Brer

Fox when he could. So Brer Fox stopped his singing and stood as still as could be, hoping that Brer Rabbit and Mr. Dog would think he was just a snowman and nothing else.

"He's stopped singing," said Brer Rabbit, looking all round in the moonlight. "I can't see anyone at all. He must have gone."

"There's only the old snowman standing there alone," said Mr. Dog." Well—he can't sing—so whoever it was must have gone."

"We'd better go into the warm again then," said Brer Rabbit. But before he could step inside, Mr. Dog caught him by the arm.

"I can smell Brer Fox," he said.

"Can you really?" said Brer Rabbit, half frightened. "Well, where can he be? Is he hiding somewhere? If he is, he's waiting around for me! I guess it must have been him after all, singing that beggar-man song."

"I'll sniff around a bit and see if I can find him," said Mr. Dog, and he ran out into the garden.

Well, Brer Fox was so frightened that he began to shiver with fear. He didn't dare to run away because he was all wrapped up in the sheet, and Mr. Dog would easily be able to catch him. So he just stood out there in the moonlight and shook from ears to toes.

Mr. Dog sniffed around the garden. He was puzzled. He could quite well smell Brer Fox—but yet he couldn't see him anywhere. It was most extraordinary.

"Heyo, Brer Rabbit," he called, "it's a funny thing but there's Brer Fox's smell around here, without Brer Fox. How do you make that out?"

Brer Rabbit couldn't make it out at all. He couldn't make out something else either. He had caught sight of the snowman shivering and shaking like a jelly, and he was most astonished.

"Mr. Dog," he called, "I think my eyes are going wrong. Seems to me as if the old snowman over there is shaking like a jelly. Do you think he's scared of you? Are snowmen scared of

144

dogs?"

"I'll bark at him and see!" said Mr. Dog and he ran right up to the snowman and barked in his loudest voice. Well, Brer Fox couldn't stand that! He gave a dreadful yell, and tore off down the garden as fast as he could go, with the white sheet all wrapped round him!

"The snowman's running away!" shouted Brer Rabbit, beside himself with delight. "The snowman's running away!"

Well, of course, Mr. Dog ran after him—and it wasn't long before he caught him either. He bit through the sheet and got hold of Brer Fox's leg.

"Let me go," yelled Brer Fox. "Let me go! Ow, let me go! I'm a poor old snowman, I am! Let me go!"

Mr. Dog gave him the worst shaking he had ever had in his life, and then let him go. The sheet was in holes, and Brer Fox's head came through one of the biggest holes as he ran. Brer

Rabbit saw it and began to laugh.

"Ho, ho, ho! You came to catch me, Brer Fox—and you got caught yourself! Ho, ho, ho! Run, Mr. Dog, run—catch him again and bite him!"

But Mr. Dog was laughing too much to run any more. The two of them watched poor Brer Fox running between the trees, stumbling over the white sheet.

"He won't build snowmen in my garden any more," said Brer Rabbit, wiping the tears off his whiskers. "No, that he won't!"

And Brer Fox never did! It took him a day and a half to mend his bitten sheet, and he was in such a bad temper that even Brer Wolf didn't dare to go near him for three weeks!

Mr. Lion Hunts for Mr. Man

MR. LION SET HIMSELF UP to be the head of all the other creatures, and he went around the neighbourhood ramping and roaring because he felt so biggitty! Everywhere he went he heard talk of Mr. Man, and the wonderful things he did.

"He's not so big as you, maybe, Mr. Lion," said Brer Rabbit, "but he's a whole lot cleverer!"

"He's not so strong as you, maybe, Mr. Lion," said Brer Bear, "but he's much more cunning."

"His voice is not so loud as yours, and his feet are not so silent, but he's twice as smart as you are, Mr. Lion," said Brer Fox.

Well, Mr. Lion didn't want to hear about Mr. Man. He wanted folks to listen to all the grand things that he, Mr. Lion, had done. But every time he began to talk biggitty someone stopped him and told him about Mr. Man.

Well, things went on like this till by and by Mr. Lion shook his big mane, he did, and let out a mighty loud roar.

"I'm going to hunt round and round, high and low to see if I can find Mr. Man," he said, "and when I find him I'll give him the sort of whacking he's never had yet! My, won't I make Mr. Man scared of Mr. Lion!"

"You'd better let Mr. Man alone," said everyone. But Mr. Lion shook his mane and set off to hunt him down.

By and by, as he was going along, with his tongue hanging out because he was so hot, he came up with Brer Steer, who was grazing along the side of the road. They bowed to one another, and then Mr. Lion asked Brer Steer some questions.

"Is there anybody round in these parts called Mr. Man?" he said.

"To be sure there is," said Brer Steer. "Anyone can tell you that. I know him very well."

"Well, then, he's the very chap I'm after!" said Mr. Lion.

"What do you want with Mr. Man?" asked Brer Steer.

"Oh, I've just come along to give him a good whacking," said Mr. Lion. "I'm going to show him who's king here!"

"Well, if that's what you've come for," said Brer Steer, "you'd better just turn yourself around, and point your nose towards home, because you'll only run yourself into pain and trouble, Mr. Lion."

"I tell you, I'm going to whack that Mr. Man," said Mr. Lion. "I've come for that, and that's what I'm a-going to do!"

Brer Steer drew a long breath and stared at Mr. Lion "You see me here, standing in front of your eyes, Mr. Lion—and you see how big I am, and what long, strong horns I've got? Well, big as my hoofs are, and sharp though my horns be, Mr. Man came out here and caught me, and put me under a yoke, and hitched me up to a cart, and made me haul his wood. He drives me anywhere he wants to. Yes, that he does. Better let Mr. Man alone, Mr. Lion. If you play about with him watch out that he doesn't hitch you up to a cart and have you prancing around carrying all his loads!"

Mr. Lion let out a roar and set out down the road. It wasn't long before he came across Brer Horse, nibbling at the grass. Mr. Lion spoke to him. "Is there anybody round these parts called Mr. Man?" he asked.

"Sure there is," said Brer Horse. "I know him mighty well, and I've been knowing him a long time, too. What do you want with Mr. Man?"

"I'm a-hunting him up so as to give him a mighty good whacking," said Mr. Lion, switching his tail about.

Brer Horse looked at Mr. Lion as if he were very sorry for him. By and by he said:

"I think you'd better let Mr. Man alone. You see how big I am, and what great strength I've got, and how tough my hoofs are? Well, this Mr. Man, he can take me and hitch me up to his cart, and make me drag him all around, and after that he can

fasten me to the plough and make me break up all his new ground. You'd better go along home, Mr. Lion. If you don't, you'll have Mr. Man making you break up his new ground for him!"

In spite of all this Mr. Lion shook his mane and said he was going to whack Mr. Man anyhow. He went on down the road and by and by he came up with Mr. Jack Sparrow. Mr. Jack Sparrow flew round Mr. Lion, and chirruped and fluttered about in surprise and admiration.

"Heyo, there!" he said. "Who would have expected to see Mr. Lion down in these parts? Where are you going, Mr. Lion?"

"I'm a-going to find Mr. Man," said Mr. Lion. "Do you know him?"

"Oh, yes," said Mr. Jack Sparrow, "I know him mighty well."

"Where is he?" asked Mr. Lion.

"He's across there in his new ground," said Mr. Jack Sparrow. "What do you want with him, Mr. Lion?"

"I'm a-going to give Mr. Man a whacking," said Mr. Lion, shaking his mane.

"You'd better let Mr. Man alone," said Mr. Jack Sparrow. "You see how little I am, and you know how high I can fly? Well, in spite of that, Mr. Man can fetch me down when he wants to! You'd better tuck your tail behind you and set out for home, Mr. Lion, in case Mr. Man fetches *you* down too!"

But Mr. Lion vowed he was going after Mr. Man, and go he would, and go he did. He hadn't ever seen Mr. Man, and he didn't know what he looked like, but he went on towards the new ground. And sure enough, there was Mr. Man, cutting up logs to make himself a new fence. He was splitting a tree-trunk in two, and as he split it, he was putting in wedges of wood to keep the split open.

He was splitting away when by and by Mr. Man heard a rustling out in the bushes, and he looked up and there was Mr. Lion.

"Howdy," said Mr. Lion. "Do you know Mr. Man?"

"I know him as well as I know my own brother!" said Mr. Man.

"I want to see this Mr. Man," said Mr. Lion, switching his tail.

"Well," said Mr. Man, with a grin, "I'll fetch him for you, if you like. But see here, Mr. Lion, you'd better just hold this tree-trunk open for me whilst I'm gone. I've got it nicely split down the middle, and I don't want the crack to close up again. Stick your paw in the crack and hold it open for me whilst I go and fetch Mr. Man."

So Mr. Lion, he marched up and slapped his paw into the crack—and then Mr. Man knocked out the wedges that kept it open, and the crack closed up, and there Mr. Lion was, caught by the paw so that he couldn't get away!

Mr. Man stood by and laughed. "If you'd been a steer or a horse, you would have run away!" he said. "And if you'd been a smart little Jack Sparrow you'd have flown off, but here you are, and you put your paw in and caught yourself!"

And with that Mr. Man went to the bushes and cut a big stick, and he whacked Mr. Lion with it till he begged for mercy. And down to this day you can't get any lion to help Mr. Man when he's splitting logs!

Brer Bear's Red Carrots

ONCE BRER BEAR had a whole field of fat red carrots. They grew there in hundreds, with their feathery green tops nodding in the breeze. Brer Rabbit thought they looked marvellous.

Now Brer Rabbit had just turned over a new leaf that week, and he felt it would be wrong to go and help himself to Brer Bear's carrots. "I must give people a chance to be kind," he said to himself. "I'll go and tell Brer Bear that I've turned over a new leaf and that I just can't let myself dig up any of his carrots without asking—and maybe he'll give me a whole lot."

So off he went to Brer Bear. Brer Bear was sitting in his front porch, basking in the sun. He wasn't very pleased to see Brer Rabbit, because he kept remembering the tricks that Brer Rabbit had played him.

"Good morning, Brer Bear," said Brer Rabbit politely. "It's a nice day, isn't it?"

"None the nicer for seeing *you*!" growled Brer Bear.

"Oh, Brer Bear! That's not a kind way to talk," said Brer Rabbit, shocked. "Why, I came to tell you that I'd turned over a new leaf!"

"About time too," said Brer Bear.

"You've a fine field of carrots," said Brer Rabbit. Brer Bear looked up at once.

"Oho! So it's my carrots you've come about," he said. "I didn't quite believe that new-leaf idea of yours, Brer Rabbit."

"Well, that's just where you are wrong," said Brer Rabbit, trying to keep his temper. "I came to tell you that if I hadn't turned over a new leaf I'd have gone and dug up your carrots without asking you, to make myself some soup. But as I've made

up my mind to be better in future, I came to ask you if I might have a few carrots. You can spare a few, surely?"

"Not to you, Brer Rabbit, not to you," said Brer Bear. "And what's more, you can't make me give you any, no matter how many new leaves you turn over! No—once a scamp, always a scamp, is what I say. And I'm not giving any carrots to you at all."

Brer Rabbit stamped away in a rage. What was the use of turning over a new leaf if he couldn't get what he wanted? No use at all! All right—he would show Brer Bear that he would *have* to give him some carrots. Yes, he'd show him!

That night Brer Rabbit took his spade and went to Brer Bear's field. He dug up a whole sackful of fine red carrots. My, they were fat and juicy! But Brer Rabbit didn't eat a single one. No—he wasn't going to do that till Brer Bear had given him some.

He hid the sack of carrots under a bush and went home. Next morning he was up bright and early and went to the bush. He dragged the sack out and took it away down the lane not far from Brer Bear's house. It was very heavy indeed. Brer Rabbit puffed and panted as he dragged it along.

He waited until he saw Brer Bear coming down the lane for his morning walk. Then he set to work to drag the sack again, puffing as if he were a train going uphill! He pretended not to see Brer Bear, and Brer Bear was mighty astonished to see Brer Rabbit dragging such a heavy sack down the lane.

"Heyo, Brer Rabbit," he said. "You seem to be too weak to take that sack along."

"Oh, Brer Bear, I've done such a foolish thing!" panted Brer Rabbit. "I've got such a lot of carrots to put in my store that I can't take them home! I shall have to leave them all here in the

lane! Oh, why didn't you give me just a few when I asked you yesterday! Now all these will go to waste, for I'll have to leave them under a bush. I can't possibly drag the sack any farther."

Brer Bear didn't think for a moment that they could be *his* carrots. He opened the neck of the sack and looked inside. Yes, there were fine fat carrots there all right. He supposed that Brer Rabbit must have gone to market and bought them.

"You can't waste carrots, Brer Rabbit," said Brer Bear. "It would be wrong."

"I know that," said Brer Rabbit. "But what am I to do?"

"I'll have them myself, if you'd like to take a few jars of honey in exchange for them," said Brer Bear, thinking that if he took the sackful it would save him the trouble of digging his own carrots that day.

"Oh, Brer Bear! How *kind* of you!" said Brer Rabbit, rubbing his whiskers in delight. "I thought yesterday that you were rude and unkind, Brer Bear. But today you are quite different. You are good and kind and generous. I like you."

Brer Bear couldn't help feeling rather pleased at this. He went into his house and brought out three jars of honey. Brer Rabbit smelt them in delight.

"*Three* jars, Brer Bear! It's more than generous of you! How mistaken I was in you! I did so long for a few of your nice carrots yesterday, but this honey is almost better than carrots—though how I *do* long for carrot soup!"

"Well—you can have a few carrots out of this sackful if you like," said Brer Bear, still feeling very generous. "Here you are— one, two, three, four, five, six, seven, eight! Nice fat ones too!"

"Brer Bear, you're a mighty good friend!" said Brer Rabbit, stuffing the carrots into his big pockets and picking up the honey. "I meant to make you give me a few of your carrots—but I didn't hope that you would give me your honey too! Good-day—and thank you!"

Brer Rabbit skipped off as merry as a grasshopper in June. Brer Bear stared after him, scratching his head. Now what did Brer Rabbit mean by saying that he would make Brer Bear give him some of his own carrots?

And then Brer Bear suddenly had a dreadful thought and he hurried off to his field as fast as his clumsy legs would take him. There he saw where Brer Rabbit had dug up a whole sackful of carrots! And how poor Brer Bear stamped and raged!

"I've given him eight of my best carrots—and three pots of my best honey! Oh, the rascal—oh, the scamp! Turning over a leaf indeed! I'd like to turn *him* over and give him a good spanking. And one of these days I will!"

But he hasn't yet! Brer Rabbit is much too clever to go near Brer Bear for a very long time.

Brer Turkey Buzzard in Trouble

NOW IT HAPPENED that Brer Turkey Buzzard once thought it would be fun to fly after Brer Rabbit and say rude things. Brer Rabbit had often tricked old Brer Buzzard, and Brer Buzzard was mighty tired of it.

So every time that Brer Rabbit went out for a walk, there was Brer Turkey Buzzard sitting on a nearby tree, waiting to squawk rude things at him.

"Heyo, Brer Rabbit, heyo, old stick-in-the-mud!" Brer Buzzard screeched. "Where's your tail? Is that all you've got for a tail! My, I'd be ashamed if that was all I'd got for a tail!"

And then Brer Buzzard would stalk around on his branch and show off his fine tail.

Another time Brer Buzzard shouted out rude things about Brer Rabbit's whiskers.

"Heyo, Brer Rabbit! How are your whiskers this morning? Is that all the whiskers you can grow? They're mighty poor!"

Brer Rabbit was angry. "Well, where are your whiskers, I'd like to know?" he yelled to Brer Buzzard.

"I sold them to a rag-and-bone man and he must have sold them to you!" squawked Brer Buzzard very rudely.

Brer Rabbit felt so angry that he made a rush at Brer Turkey Buzzard—but Brer Buzzard just sailed into the air, squawking with laughter.

Then Brer Rabbit tried pretending not to hear when Brer Buzzard called after him—but that wasn't much good, because Brer Buzzard only became ruder and ruder, and soon there was quite a crowd of creatures following Brer Rabbit just to laugh at the bad things Brer Buzzard said!

Well, pretty soon Brer Rabbit began to think hard about all

this. He wasn't used to being treated in such a way—and the worst of it was he couldn't get hold of Brer Buzzard, because he just rose into the air as soon as Brer Rabbit got near him!

At last Brer Rabbit thought of an idea. He shut himself up in his house for two days and gave out that he had a bad cold. Then, on the third day, he went out with his head all wrapped up in a shawl and a thick coat round his shoulders. He sniffed as he went, and sneezed into a big yellow handkerchief.

Brer Turkey Buzzard was waiting for him as usual. He had had time to think of a few more quite new rude things. He opened his beak as Brer Rabbit came out.

"Heyo, Brer Rabbit!" he squawked. "Why don't you buy a little honey to make you sweet? You look mighty sour to-day!"

Brer Rabbit took no notice. Brer Turkey Buzzard shouted even more loudly. Brer Rabbit looked round as if he heard something.

"Did you speak to me, Brer Buzzard?" he asked politely. "My cold must have made me deaf."

He sat down by the roadside. Brer Turkey Buzzard flew down to a nearby tree and shouted again.

"I'm sure you must be saying something very interesting," said Brer Rabbit, putting his paw behind one ear as if to hear better. "But I'm hard of hearing today. Is it anything important you have to say?"

"Why don't you wash behind your ears?" cried Brer Buzzard rudely.

"Why don't I lend you my shears?" said Brer Rabbit, looking rather surprised. "What do you want my shears for? To cut off your tail?"

"I said, 'Why don't you wash behind your *ears*?" shouted Brer Buzzard, hopping to the ground.

"Really, Brer Buzzard, you must think me very rude," said Brer Rabbit, unwrapping the shawl from his head. "I'm deaf both sides, it seems. Could you speak a little louder."

Brer Buzzard hopped nearer and squawked even more loudly.

Brer Rabbit shook his head politely and put a paw behind *both* ears. "You'll have to shout right into my ears, I'm afraid," he said. "I can't seem to hear a thing."

Brer Turkey Buzzard hopped right up and leaned over Brer Rabbit's big ears.

"Why don't you wash behind..." he began to shout—but that's as far as he got. As quick as lightning Brer Rabbit flung the shawl over Brer Buzzard's head and held him tight!

Brer Buzzard kicked out with his feet and struck with his wings—but he couldn't see because his head was in the shawl. He began to squawk loudly.

"Now, now," said Brer Rabbit, shaking him. "That's not the way to talk. In fact, Brer Buzzard, it strikes me that you don't know how to talk politely at all! I think I'd better teach you. Now what was it you said about my tail the other day? Something rude, I know."

Brer Buzzard said nothing. He was afraid of repeating anything now.

"Yes—I remember. You said you'd be ashamed if you had a tail like mine! Well, well, Brer Buzzard, I'm sure you won't mind giving me a few of your tail-feathers to make myself a tail as grand as yours!"

And what did old Brer Rabbit do but whip a big handful of feathers out of Brer Turkey Buzzard's tail! Brer Buzzard gave a loud squawk. Brer Rabbit unwrapped the shawl and let him go.

"Thanks for the new tail," said Brer Rabbit, and he began to tie the tail-feathers neatly on to his own bobtail. "I shall tell everyone how kind you've been to me, Brer Buzzard! Do keep near to me so that every one can see you've given me your tail!"

Brer Buzzard took a look at his own poor tail and gave a squawk of dismay. He flew off in shame to hide himself—but old Brer Rabbit, he paraded about with a long tail of fine buzzard-feathers for weeks after that!

And Brer Turkey Buzzard was mighty polite to him when he met him again. He knew it wasn't any good trying to get the better of Brer Rabbit!

Brer Rabbit's Apple Tree

NOW ONCE BRER BEAR and Brer Fox put their heads together and made up their minds to catch Brer Rabbit the very next time they saw him.

"That tiresome creature is always up to tricks," complained Brer Bear.

"But this time we'll have him, and he won't escape!" grinned Brer Fox. "He'll be going along through his orchard this evening. We'll wait there and catch him!"

"Where shall I meet you?" asked Brer Bear.

"Under the tree in the middle of the orchard," said Brer Fox. "Good-bye till then!"

So that evening, a little while before Brer Rabbit was due to stroll through his orchard, Brer Fox turned up. He went to the middle tree, and sat down with his back to the trunk.

It was an apple tree and the apples were ripe. The evening was windy, and as the breeze blew, an apple became too heavy for its stalk and fell off.

Thud! It fell right on to Brer Fox's head and gave him a terrible shock. He blinked his eyes and looked round. Who was throwing things at him? He would soon show them what happened to people who hit him like that!

Another apple fell, thud! This time it hit him on his long nose, and Brer Fox leapt up in pain. He looked wildly round, but not a soul could he see. Then a third apple fell and knocked his left ear quite flat. Brer Fox gave a howl of rage and ran round and round the tree to see who was throwing apples at him. He never once thought that he was sitting under an apple tree!

"Ho! So somebody is hiding, and having a nice little game with me!" thought Brer Fox. "Well, I'll hide too—and when I see who it is I'll pounce out on them and bite their ears off!"

So he hid behind a bush and waited. But nobody came. Then, after a while, Brer Bear shuffled up to meet old Brer Fox. He sat down under the apple tree, lifted up his head and yawned widely.

And at that very moment a big apple fell off the tree, right into his mouth, and almost choked him! Brer Bear coughed and choked, and the apple shot out of his mouth again. Brer Bear sat up in anger.

"Now who's flinging apples at me!" he grunted. "Why, I might have choked to death! Just wait till I see who it is."

Bump! A large apple fell on to his forehead and another on his shoulder. Brer Bear jumped up in a rage. He stood there, watching and waiting to see who it was that was throwing apples so hard at him.

Now old Brer Rabbit left his house just about that time, and he made his way through the orchard. He kept his eyes and ears wide open, as he always did, and before long he saw some footprints in a muddy patch.

"Ha!" said Brer Rabbit, stopping and scratching his chin. "Those are Brer Fox's footmarks. Now what is he waiting about here for? I'll go carefully."

So he went very carefully and quietly, and before long he spied old Brer Fox hiding behind the bush, watching out to see who had thrown apples at him. Brer Fox didn't see Brer Rabbit. Brer Rabbit tiptoed away, and presently he spied Brer Bear standing under the apple tree, looking as angry as a hen left out in the rain.

"Now what's the matter with *him!*" wondered Brer Rabbit. And then he guessed! A large apple suddenly fell from the tree and hit Brer Bear on his blunt snout. He gave a yell and rubbed his nose.

"Wait till I see the person that's throwing things at me!" growled Brer Bear, looking all around. Brer Rabbit grinned a little to himself, and then he walked boldly up to Brer Bear.

"Is someone throwing things at you?" he asked. "What a shame! I believe I know who it is! I spied them hiding behind a bush just now. Brer Bear, you just tiptoe round behind that clump of bushes over there, and you'll see who it is hiding! Take a few apples with you, and throw them hard at *him!* That will teach him to play tricks on you."

Brer Bear glared at Brer Rabbit. Then he picked up a handful of apples and went on tiptoe round the clump of bushes. Brer Rabbit followed close behind, grinning to himself. When Brer Bear spied Brer Fox crouching low down on the ground he nearly burst with rage.

"So it was Brer Fox who threw things at me!" he growled, deep down in his throat. "Well, I'll teach him how to throw!"

And with that Brer Bear flung an apple at Brer Fox as hard as

ever he could! Brer Fox got the apple in the very middle of his back, and it hurt him. He sprang up in rage and turned to see who it was. When he saw Brer Bear just about to throw yet another apple at him, he shouted angrily and ran towards him.

"So it was you who threw apples at me when I was waiting for you under the tree! That's a funny thing to do to a friend! Weren't we going to catch Brer Rabbit! And you go and spoil everything by flinging apples about! Wait till I catch you!"

"I'll teach you to throw apples at me!" roared Brer Bear, who was now in a fine old temper too. "I was sitting under that tree waiting for you, as quiet as could be—and plonk, along came an apple and hit me hard! I'm just getting a bit of my own back now. Take that—and that!"

Brer Fox got the apples on his head, and he gave a shout of rage. He sprang on Brer Bear and got him down. They rolled over and over on the grass. Then Brer Bear got on top and bit

Brer Fox on the right ear. Brer Fox was so annoyed that he tried his very hardest to get hold of Brer Bear's little tail and pull it out!

Well, the one who enjoyed that fight most of all was old Brer Rabbit. He just sat and cracked his sides with laughing! Then a great idea came to him. He ran to fill his pockets with the rottenest apples he could find.

And soon he was pelting Brer Fox and Brer Bear with them as hard as ever he could! Plonk, splish, plonk! Those apples hit them hard and then burst into juice all over them.

Brer Bear and Brer Fox got up and stared round. They saw old Brer Rabbit sitting on the fence, almost falling off with laughter.

"It must have been Brer Rabbit pelting us with apples!" said Brer Bear. "What sillies we are! Here we came along to catch him and eat him for our dinner—and all we do is to fight one another and roll on the ground whilst he throws his rotten apples at us! Quick—catch him!"

But Brer Rabbit didn't wait to be caught! He was off and away long before either Brer Bear or Brer Fox had reached the fence. And by the time they reached his house the door was bolted and all the windows were shut.

"Go and make yourselves into apple-pie!" yelled Brer Rabbit's voice from a window. "I'll make some custard to go with it!"

But he didn't, of course, though he would dearly have liked to! Cheeky old Brer Rabbit!

Brer Fox Goes to Market

ONCE BRER FOX and Brer Rabbit very badly wanted some money, and they tried to plan how to get some.

"We could go and dig in Mr. Man's field and earn some," said Brer Rabbit.

"Pooh!" said Brer Fox. "That's too much like hard work! Think again, Brer Rabbit, think again!"

"Well, we could find a bee-tree, collect the honey, and take it to market," said Brer Rabbit.

"And get stung all over," said Brer Fox. "You are not very bright today, Brer Rabbit."

"Well, you take a turn at thinking, then," said Brer Rabbit crossly. "I'm getting a headache with thinking so much."

"I've got a fine idea," said Brer Fox. "What about going along to Brer Bear's house when he's gone out and taking a few things to sell at the market?"

"But that's stealing," said Brer Rabbit, quite shocked.

"Well, it would do Brer Bear good to lose a few of his things," said Brer Fox. "But if you think it would be stealing from him, what about going to Miss Goose's house and taking a few of her things? She's got some nice sheets and towels we could sell at the market."

"But that would be stealing too," said Brer Rabbit. "Don't be silly, Brer Fox."

"Now if you're going to call everything stealing, I shall stop thinking of plans," said Brer Fox, and he showed his teeth.

"All right, all right," said Brer Rabbit in a hurry. "We'll have your plan. But who does the taking? I don't want to."

"Of course you'll have to," said Brer Fox. "I'll do the selling— and you must do the taking."

"Well, does it matter whose house I go to?" asked Brer Rabbit.

"Not a bit," said Brer Fox. "Go to anyone's you like."

"And you are quite, quite sure it won't be stealing?" asked Brer Rabbit.

"Quite, quite sure," said Brer Fox. "Now see you get into someone's house, choose a few things, bring them to me here— and I'll go to market with them. I'll sell them, and you shall have half the money. I promise you that."

"Thank you kindly," said Brer Rabbit. "I'll go straight away, Brer Fox. But mind you stay here till I come back, so that I will know where to find you!"

"I'll stay all right," said Brer Fox with a grin. "Hurry now."

Brer Rabbit hurried off, grinning away to himself. He didn't go to Brer Bear's. He didn't go to Miss Goose's. No—he went to Brer Fox's own house. It was quite empty, of course. Brer Rabbit pushed open the door and looked around.

He took all the spoons and forks out of the drawer. He took all the clean white towels out of the cupboard. He took six pots of jam from the larder. He took a brand-new kettle from the stove. That was enough for him to carry, so he hurried back with all his goods to where Brer Fox was waiting impatiently.

"Good!" said Brer Fox, taking all the things. "Now I'll be off to the market and sell all these for as good a price as I can get."

"You are quite, quite sure it wasn't stealing?" said Brer Rabbit.

"Oh, quite sure," said Brer Fox. "You make me tired, asking that question over and over again. Stay here till I come back and I'll give you your share of the money."

He went off to market. He stood there and offered the spoons and forks for sale, the nice white towels, the brand-new kettle, and the six pots of jam.

He wasn't long in selling them, for he didn't ask very high prices. Soon he had ten shillings in his pocket, and he hurried back to Brer Rabbit.

"Look here!" he said. "Ten shillings between us! Five for you and five for me."

"Thanks very much indeed," said Brer Rabbit, putting his money into his pocket. "I'll walk home with you, Brer Fox."

So the two of them walked back to Brer Fox's house

together—and, of course, as soon as Brer Fox got indoors, he saw that six pots of jam had gone from his larder, that his kettle and spoons and forks were missing, and that there were no nice white towels in his cupboard.

"Hi-yi!" he yelled in a temper. "Someone's been here and taken my things! Wait till I catch the thief! Just wait! What else has he stolen? Oh, the scamp! Oh, the robber!"

"What has been stolen?" asked Brer Rabbit, keeping the other side of the gate. "How strange, Brer Fox—just the very things you sold at the market this morning! Now don't you think that's really VERY peculiar!"

Brer Fox turned and stared at Brer Rabbit, who was grinning all over his whiskery face! Brer Fox went quite green. He spoke to Brer Rabbit in a shaking voice.

"Brer Rabbit——whose house did you go to for those things I sold at the market?"

"Why, yours," said Brer Rabbit. "You said it didn't matter whose house I went to. Didn't you mean what you said, Brer Fox?"

Brer Fox gave such a dreadful yell that Brer Rabbit thought it was time to run, and run he did! My, how he ran! But when he got to the top of the hill he stopped and turned round.

"Hie, Brer Fox!" he called. "Are you still quite sure it wasn't stealing?"

And old Brer Fox hadn't anything to say to that!

Brer Rabbit and the Guy

ONCE BRER WOLF and Brer Fox put their heads together and laid a plan to catch Old Brer Rabbit.

"It will be Guy Fawkes Day soon," said Brer Fox. "What about me dressing up as a guy, and you wheeling me through the streets till we see Brer Rabbit. He's sure to want to come and look at the guy—and I'll pounce on him straight away!"

"That's a good idea, Brer Fox," said Brer Wolf. "We'll do that!"

So when Guy Fawkes Day came, Brer Wolf dressed Brer Fox up in old clothes, and put a mask on his face. It was a funny mask, with a broad smile on it. Brer Fox's sharp eyes looked through the holes, and how he grinned to himself to think of Brer Rabbit coming up close to him! Wouldn't he pounce on him!

Brer Wolf put Brer Fox into a chair with wheels on it, so that he could wheel him easily through the streets.

"Now don't you sit up too straight," he warned Brer Fox, "else you won't look like a guy. Go all crooked in the chair, as guys do. Try to look as if you are stuffed with saw-dust."

So Brer Fox slumped himself down in the chair, and leaned all crooked to make himself look like a real guy. And Brer Wolf took the handles of the wheel-chair and wheeled him away to the village.

Pretty soon they met old Brer Terrapin, and he raised himself up to have a look at the guy. But he was too small to see much further than the guy's feet. He stared at those for a long time. The guy had on a pair of very old boots, and one boot had a hole in it—and through the hole Brer Terrapin felt sure he could see brown fur.

"Brown fur!" thought Brer Terrapin to himself in surprise. "That's strange. That guy isn't a real guy. It's somebody dressed up to look like one."

Old Brer Terrapin ambled on his way, and pretty soon he met Brer Rabbit skipping along as merry as a blackbird in spring.

"Heyo, Brer Rabbit," called Brer Terrapin. "Have you seen the guy that Brer Wolf is wheeling around?"

"No," said Brer Rabbit. "I haven't. I'll go and have a look at it."

"Well, don't you go too close, that's all," said Brer Terrapin. "That guy had got brown fur on his ankles!"

Brer Rabbit grinned. "So old Brer Fox is up to tricks, is he?" he said. "Well, you come along with me, Brer Terrapin, and we'll see what we can do about it."

So the two of them went along to where Brer Wolf stood behind the guy's chair. Brer Rabbit called out to him.

"Brer Wolf! You're wanted at home for a minute! I'll take the guy for you till you come back."

Now this sounded good to Brer Wolf. If he left Brer Rabbit in charge of the guy, what could be easier than for Brer Fox to jump out of the chair and catch him!

"Right!" said Brer Wolf. "I'll go home and see what's wanted. I'll be back in a few minutes, Brer Rabbit. Just stand quietly by the guy. That's all you have to do. And remember to shout, 'Guy! Guy! A penny for the guy!' when anyone comes by. That's my cap down there on the ground for people to throw pennies into."

"Right!" said Brer Rabbit, seeing that two or three people were coming along. "You go now, Brer Wolf. Hurry!"

Brer Fox didn't like to jump at Brer Rabbit with Brer Goat and Brer Possum coming by. So he just sat slumped down in the chair, waiting for them to pass.

"Heyo, Brer Goat!" cried Brer Rabbit. "Can you help me with this guy? He can't sit up properly, and I'm afraid he'll fall out of the chair."

"Yes, I'll help you," said Brer Goat, and he came up. "What do you want me to do?"

"Oh, just hold him for me whilst I get him fixed," said Brer Rabbit, winking at old Brer Terrapin who was standing not far off, splitting his sides with trying not to laugh. Brer Rabbit whipped out some rope from his pocket and Brer Goat took hold of the guy to pull him straight in the chair.

And before Brer Fox could do anything about it, he found himself tied tightly to the back of the chair so that he couldn't move!

"Thanks, Brer Goat!" said Brer Rabbit. "Now he's all right!"

Then Brer Rabbit began to wheel the guy down the street shouting, "Guy, guy, a penny for the guy!"

Brer Fox didn't like it at all. He began to struggle and wriggle for all he was worth, and the passers-by stared in surprise.

"It's a live guy!" they said in astonishment; "Who have you got there, Brer Rabbit?"

"Oh, I've got Brer Fox!" said Brer Rabbit. "He's been a bit of a nuisance to me lately, so I thought I'd pay him out. I'm making him into a guy—doesn't it suit him!"

Well, Brer Fox was simply furious. He struggled with all his might to get free, but the rope held him tightly.

People laughed to see Brer Fox trying to get away. They thought Brer Rabbit was mighty clever to catch him like that! They threw pennies to Brer Rabbit and he sent Brer Terrapin to buy some rockets at a shop.

"We'll take him to a bonfire and send him up in the air with the rockets," grinned Brer Rabbit. Brer Fox was very frightened to hear this.

"Help ! Help!" he yelled. "Brer Wolf! Where are you?"

Well, Brer Rabbit wheeled Brer Fox to a big pile of rubbish, and he tied four rockets to him. "Light the bonfire," he said to Brer Terrapin, with a wink. "We'll make things hot for Brer Fox, so we will!"

Brer Rabbit didn't really mean to burn Brer Fox, but Brer Fox didn't know that. He yelled so loudly that Brer Wolf heard him. Brer Wolf had been home and found that he wasn't wanted at all. He had guessed that it was a trick of Brer Rabbit's to get

him away, so he had hurried back. But by that time Brer Rabbit had wheeled away Brer Fox, and Brer Wolf didn't know where.

But when he heard Brer Fox yelling, he ran to save him. Brer Rabbit saw him coming. He quickly lighted the ends of the rockets and then he and Brer Terrapin scurried away behind a bush.

"Save me, save me!" squealed Brer Fox, hearing the rockets sizzle behind him, where Brer Rabbit had tied them to the chair. He wriggled hard and the chair fell over on top of him. The rockets went off with a loud bang, and two of them flew straight at Brer Wolf.

"Ker-plunk!" They hit him and bowled him over. What a shock they gave him! He got up, turned and ran with all his might, yelling out, "Brer Fox has shot me! Brer Fox has shot me!"

The rope that bound Brer Fox broke and Brer Fox was free. But did he go chasing Brer Rabbit? Not he! He had had enough of that rascally rabbit for weeks to come. And my—you should have heard Brer Terrapin and Brer Rabbit laugh! It would have given you a fit of the giggles too!

Brer Rabbit and the Little Girl

ONE DAY, after Brer Rabbit had been tramping all around to find some salad to make his dinner good, he came near to Mr. Man's house. He went along until he came to a little gate, and near the garden gate he saw a little girl playing around in the sun.

Well, Brer Rabbit looked in through the garden-gate, and saw cabbages and lettuces and carrots and all kinds of other greens growing there, and his mouth began to water.

He took a walk up to the little girl, bowed politely, and talked mighty nicely to her.

"Howdy, Little Girl," said Brer Rabbit. "How do you feel this morning?"

"Howdy, Brer Rabbit," said the little girl. "How are you feeling yourself?"

"Poorly, Little Girl, poorly," said Brer Rabbit. "Tell me, are you the little girl whose Pa lives up in the big white house?"

"Yes, I'm the little girl whose Pa lives in that big white house you can see yonder," said the little girl.

"Then I'm mighty glad to hear that," said Brer Rabbit, "because I've just been to see your Pa, and he sent me to tell his little girl to open the garden-gate for me so that I can go in to get a few greens."

"I'll open the gate now," said the little girl, and she ran to open the gate, and with that Brer Rabbit hopped in, and got a fine armful of greens and then hopped out again.

He bowed politely when he left the little girl, and said he was much obliged to her. Then he set out for home, and made himself a fine dinner that day.

Well, the next day Brer Rabbit hid near the garden gate again, and when he saw the little girl come out to play he ran

up to her, told her the same tale as before, and she let him into the garden. He picked all he wanted of the greens, and then set out for home again.

This seemed a mighty easy way of getting greens, and Brer Rabbit, he went up to the garden every day for a long time and the little girl let him in. Things went on like this till Mr. Man began to miss his greens, and he kept on missing them, and got so angry that he began to blame everybody on the place for taking them.

When the little girl heard this she went to him and said: "My goodness, Pa, didn't you tell Mr. Rabbit to ask me to let him into the garden each day to get some greens, and haven't I done it every day since!"

When Mr. Man heard that, he was mighty wild. Then he began to laugh, and he told the little girl he had forgotten all about Mr. Rabbit.

"Now, Little Girl, next time Mr. Rabbit comes along, you take him into the garden as usual, and then you run as fast as you can and tell me he's there, because I've got some business to do with that young fellow that must be attended to."

So the next morning, when Brer Rabbit came up, the little girl let him into the garden, and then she ran up to the house and shouted: "Oh, Pa! Pa! Oh, Pa! Here is Brer Rabbit, in the garden this minute! Here he is, Pa!"

Then Mr. Man rushed out and grabbed a fishing-line that was hanging in the back-porch, and he ran to the garden and when he got there he saw Brer Rabbit trampling round on the strawberry bed and smashing down all the tomatoes too. Brer Rabbit saw Mr. Man and squatted down behind a cabbage, but it wasn't any use. Mr. Man saw him all right, and before Brer Rabbit could count three Mr. Man had caught him and tied him up hard and fast with the fishing-line. After he had got him well tied up Mr. Man took a step back and grinned at Brer Rabbit.

"You've tricked me lots of times, Brer Rabbit, but this time I've tricked you! I'm going to give you such a whacking! And then I'm going to skin you, see? And to make sure you get the right sort of whacking I'm just a-going to step up to the house and fetch my little red cowhide whip!"

Before he went to get his whip Mr. Man called to the little girl.

"You watch Brer Rabbit for me whilst I'm gone," he said.

Brer Rabbit didn't say a word till Mr. Man was out of the gate. Then he began to sing. And in those days it was a real treat to hear Brer Rabbit sing.

The song he sang went like this:

> *The jay-bird hunts for the sparrow's nest;*
> *The kestrel sails all around;*
> *The squirrel, he jumps from the top of the tree;*
> *Mr. Mole, he stays in the ground;*
> *He hides and he stays till the dew drops down;*
> *Mr. Mole, he hides in the ground!*

When the little girl heard this song she laughed, and asked Brer Rabbit to sing some more. But Brer Rabbit began to cough, and he shook his head.

"Seems I've got something in my throat," said Brer Rabbit. "I can't sing any more."

"Oh, do, do, do!" begged the little girl. "Please do, Brer Rabbit. That was a beautiful song."

"I can dance much better than I can sing," said Brer Rabbit.

"Well, dance then, do dance," begged the little girl.

"Now tell me, how in the name of goodness do you think I can dance when I'm all tied up like this!" said Brer Rabbit.

"Well, I'll untie you, and then you can dance for me," said the little girl.

"All right, you do that," said Brer Rabbit. "Then I can do a fine dance for you."

So the little girl untied him, and Brer Rabbit, he sort of stretched himself and looked all round.

And then he began to dance! Yes, old Brer Rabbit put his feet together and he danced a mighty fine dance! He danced down the path, he did, and he danced right out of the garden gate. And old Brer Rabbit didn't stop dancing till he got home. My, that was a mighty fine dance Brer Rabbit did that day!

178